THE CIRCLE OF
FOOTPRINTS

SUDDENLY A GIRL'S TERRIFIED SCREAM PIERCED
THE AIR.

The Circle of Footprints   *Frontispiece (Page 43)*

THE DANA GIRLS MYSTERY STORIES

THE CIRCLE OF FOOTPRINTS

BY

CAROLYN KEENE

Author of

THE NANCY DREW MYSTERY STORIES

NEW YORK

GROSSET & DUNLAP

PUBLISHERS

CONTENTS

THE CIRCLE OF FOOTPRINTS

CHAPTER I

DISTURBING NEWS

"OH, Louise! I have startling news!"

Jean Dana, waving a local newspaper in one hand, came hurrying into the study room which she shared with Louise, her sister, at Starhurst School. The dark-haired girl seated at the window and absorbed in the contents of a text book, smiled as she glanced up. By nature she was rather tranquil, unlike the fair-haired, tempestuous Jean, and had learned from experience that her sister became excited over trifles.

"What's happened now?" she then inquired calmly.

"Oh, Louise, how can you be so placid? Just look at this item in the Record!"

"I can't when you're waving it around," Louise laughed. "What does it say?"

"There's been a strange steamship accident at sea. The *Balaska*——"

1

"Uncle Ned's ship!" Louise exclaimed in alarm. "Quick! Let me see that paper!"

"I thought you'd get excited," Jean replied, indicating the item which appeared on the front page. "But there's no need for worry. The *Balaska* is still afloat and Uncle Ned wasn't among those injured."

Quickly Louise scanned the newspaper story. She had nearly finished reading it when Evelyn Starr, chum and schoolmate of the Dana girls, appeared in the doorway. Evelyn was a popular student at the boarding school and enjoyed a unique distinction, since at one time the property had belonged to her family.

"I hope I'm not interrupting," she apologized. "I noticed the door was open and—why, is anything wrong?"

"Yes."

"What is it?"

"Several passengers were injured on Uncle Ned's ship," Jean explained. "Oh, it wasn't his fault. A reckless aviator was flying over the *Balaska,* and according to the newspaper account the plane dived low to salute one of the passengers. It crashed on deck when its motors failed."

"How dreadful!" Evelyn shuddered. "Was anyone killed?"

"Fortunately not," Louise answered, reading on. "Three passengers sustained minor injuries. The airplane pilot was the most seriously hurt. He isn't expected to live."

"What is his name?"

Jean glanced at the newspaper story again before replying. Then she answered:

"Mason Doke. I've never heard of him."

"Why, I have!" Evelyn cried. "At least, I've heard of a man by that name."

"Then he must be a well-known flier," Louise commented.

Evelyn smiled disdainfully. "He was flying high in finance when I learned about him. Mason Doke forged a check in my brother's name and it caused all sorts of trouble. The matter was finally straightened out. Franklin never prosecuted the man."

"Do you suppose the forger could have been this reckless aviator?" Jean asked curiously.

"I have no idea. Mason Doke isn't a common name."

"Well, whoever he is, he has caused Captain Ned plenty of trouble," Louise said. "Think of all those injured passengers, not to mention the damage done to the steamship."

"I hope the company officials won't blame Uncle Ned," Jean commented anxiously.

"Why should they?" her sister questioned. "He had nothing to do with the accident. He couldn't keep that fellow from flying over the ship."

"Of course it wasn't Uncle Ned's fault," Jean agreed, "but it's a pity the accident occurred. It gives the ship unfavorable publicity."

"This newspaper account isn't a very detailed one," Louise frowned. "I suppose we'll hear more about the accident when the *Balaska* docks in New York. Or possibly Uncle Ned will send us a cable before he gets in."

Not infrequently the Dana girls received messages from Captain Ned Dana when he was at sea. After every severe storm he considerately assured them of his safety, sending similar dispatches to his sister, Harriet Dana. She resided at Oak Falls, where she, her brother, and the two nieces made their home. It was some little distance from Penfield, the site of the exclusive Starhurst School for Girls.

"I really dropped in to find out if you have given up that shopping trip," Evelyn remarked to her friends after the subject of the steamship accident had been exhausted. "You spoke of running in to town this afternoon, you know."

Jean glanced quickly at the clock. "We haven't given up the idea, but if we're going we'll have to start at once. You'll come with us, Evelyn?"

"I'd like to. I have some things to buy."

While the Dana girls changed their frocks,

Evelyn ran back to her room for a hat. She joined them a few minutes later in the lower hall.

The three friends were just leaving the building when a uniformed messenger boy came toward them, a yellow envelope in his hand.

"Oh, wait a minute," Jean said impulsively to her companions. "I'm sure that boy has a radiogram for either Louise or me. It must be from Captain Ned!"

She hurried forward to ask the boy for the wire.

"You are Lettie Briggs?" he inquired politely.

Jean became slightly confused and stammered, "Oh, no! I thought you had a message for Louise or Jean Dana."

"One would think you two girls were the only persons of importance in this dormitory!" a familiar, contemptuous voice cut into the conversation.

Jean whirled about to find herself face to face with the Briggs girl.

"I'm sorry, Lettie," she apologized. "Louise and I were expecting a message from Uncle Ned, and——"

"Don't trouble yourself to explain," Lettie interrupted aloofly. "I guess no great harm has been done since you didn't open the envelope."

Jean flushed angrily. "Of course I didn't open it. I merely inquired——"

"I'll take the wire," Lettie cut her off again, addressing the boy.

She signed for the message and walked a few paces away to open it. The Dana girls saw her stare coldly at them as if to imply that she thought Jean might attempt to steal a glance over her shoulder.

"How I detest that girl!" Jean said in a tense undertone. "She deliberately misconstrues everything I do or say."

"Everyone at Starhurst dislikes Lettie," Evelyn added feelingly. "But I suppose she can't help having such a mean disposition."

"Lettie doesn't receive a telegram often," Louise smiled. "This is a great event for her. I hope she enjoys it."

Obviously the Briggs girl had not been the recipient of good news. She uttered a distressed cry as she read the message. Evelyn and the Dana girls asked her what was wrong.

"My father has been injured," Lettie proclaimed in a dramatic voice, addressing a group of schoolmates who were emerging from the building at that moment.

"Oh, I'm sorry," Louise said sympathetically. "Not seriously, I hope."

"How did it happen?" Jean inquired.

Lettie whirled upon her with blazing eyes.

"*You* should ask! My father was injured while sailing on that old wreck of a ship called the *Balaska*. If your Uncle Ned had known anything about managing a vessel, this wouldn't have happened!"

"Do you know just what did occur?" Jean demanded coldly.

"No, I don't. But my father is hurt and it was your Uncle Ned's fault!"

"The accident wasn't his fault at all," Louise broke in. She thrust a copy of the afternoon paper into Lettie's hand. "Just read this and you'll see."

"Your father's name wasn't mentioned in the story so his injuries are very likely slight," Jean added.

Lettie read the newspaper account reluctantly. When she had finished her eyes still burned with unreasoning anger.

"I don't care what this story says! I know it was all Captain Dana's fault. He isn't fit to be a sea captain—he's a blundering, incompetent——"

"Girls! Girls!" a voice remonstrated from directly behind. "What is the meaning of this? Lettie, what are you saying about Captain Dana?"

Everyone turned to see Mrs. Crandall, the headmistress of the school, standing in the doorway. She came quickly down the steps.

Louise and Jean apologized for the scene which had been created, even though it was not of their making, and showed Mrs. Crandall the newspaper. To their amazement she leaned weakly back against one of the stone pillars.

"This is dreadful," she murmured. "Mason Doke is my nephew!"

"Your nephew?" Louise gasped.

Mrs. Crandall nodded as she re-read the newspaper story.

"I must show this account to Professor Crandall," she said.

Trying to hide her distress, Mrs. Crandall turned to leave. Then she remembered that she had not settled the unfortunate argument between Lettie and the Dana girls.

"I am sorry about your father, Lettie," she said kindly. "I realize that you are greatly upset over the accident, otherwise you would not have said the things you did. Captain Dana is an excellent officer and obviously was not at fault in this matter."

"Yes, Mrs. Crandall," Lettie murmured, avoiding the woman's glance.

"I think you owe the Dana girls an apology."

"Yes, Mrs. Crandall," Lettie muttered.

The headmistress went inside the building. The instant her back was turned, Lettie glared hatefully at the Dana girls. She had no inten-

tion of apologizing. Instead, she too walked
away.

"That girl—" Jean began, but her sister
caught her by the hand, pulling her toward the
street.

"You may as well forget it, Jean. Here
comes our bus. We'll have to run."

The three girls boarded the vehicle, and in a
short time found themselves in the shopping
section of Penfield. Jean and Louise each
bought a new brown felt hat and afterward
helped Evelyn select a costume for a special
dancing class.

"Let's drop in at Reni's for a soda," Louise
proposed as they left the store. "It's just
around the corner."

The girls approached the sweet shop, a fa-
vorite haunt of Starhurst students. Suddenly
Louise halted. Her attention had been drawn
toward a uniformed boy who was tinkering
with his bicycle at the curb.

"Isn't that the lad who called at the school
with Lettie's telegram, Jean?"

The boy glanced up just then and the girls
nodded and smiled. They would have passed
on without speaking had they not observed that
he seemed greatly upset.

"Having trouble?" Louise inquired kindly.

"I've had two flat tires since I left Starhurst," the boy answered in a discouraged

tone. "I'm late getting back to the office. That means I'll probably be fired."

"Perhaps you can find a better job," Evelyn remarked encouragingly.

The boy shook his head. "Jobs are hard to get. I can't afford to be without one even for a week. I don't make much as it is, but we need every penny at home."

"Your father is out of work?" Louise inquired with sympathy.

The boy gave a short, bitter laugh. "We haven't had any help from him—not in a long while. When the going got hard he just disappeared. I wish I could find him. I'd make him support Mother and my kid sisters."

"How many are there in your family?" Jean asked.

"I have two sisters, Belle and Daisy. They're mighty nice kids, too. Belle is four now and Daisy is just a few months over five."

"And you provide the entire support for the family?" Louise inquired in wonder and admiration.

The boy nodded. "Such as it is. We don't have any too much to eat some of the time. I don't mind about myself because I'm strong, but my sisters need plenty of milk."

"You haven't told us your name," Louise said quietly.

"It's Joe. Joe Doke."

The Dana girls wondered if they had heard correctly.

"What is your father's first name?" Louise inquired.

"Mason. Mason Doke."

"Well, of all things," Evelyn began, but the Dana girls sent her a warning glance.

Before they could ask whether or not he was an aviator, a huge truck came careening around the corner at a high rate of speed. It skidded toward the curb.

Evelyn screamed, and with the Dana girls sprang back toward safety. Louise caught Joe by the arm, dragging him with them. It was an act which saved the boy's life.

The truck swung wide from its normal path and crashed into the bicycle, completely demolishing it. The driver slackened his speed, then hastened on again.

Joe Doke surveyed the wreckage in stunned dismay. Then the full meaning of the disaster overwhelmed him and he began to sob convulsively. Louise tried to comfort the lad but he refused to be consoled.

"Now I know I'll be discharged," he murmured brokenly. "Poor Mother! And the kids! Whatever will become of them?"

CHAPTER II

A Tin Box

EVEN a casual glance disclosed that Joe Doke's bicycle was completely demolished. It was bent and twisted beyond repair.

"That reckless truck driver might have killed us all," Jean cried angrily. "He ought to pay for the wheel. Did you get the license number, Louise?"

"No, I didn't," her sister confessed regretfully. "The truck was traveling too fast."

Joe and the girls were staring disconsolately at the wreckage and did not observe a middle-aged, stern-faced man until he halted beside them.

"So here you are, Joe," he said sarcastically. "I might have known I'd find you loitering as usual. You seem to think we pay you to have a good time gadding around with the girls!"

"I wasn't loitering, Mr. Cohan," the messenger boy insisted earnestly. "Honestly I wasn't. I had two flats on the way back from Starhurst, and then the truck smashed into my bicycle."

"Wrecking your wheel is absolutely the last

12

straw!'' the telegraph company manager said
heatedly. ''No, don't try to tell me how it happened. You're through. Do you understand?
Fired!''

''Please, Mr. Cohan——''

''Not a word. I've had enough of your excuses. Here is your pay to date.'' The man
took two dollars from his pocket and thrust
them into Joe's hand.

''Mr. Cohan, I think you're making a mistake,'' Louise said politely. ''The boy is telling
you the truth. He wasn't loitering——''

''Young lady, I am not interested in your
opinion.''

''You're not giving the boy a fair deal,''
Jean interposed.

''I run my department as I like!'' Mr. Cohan
snapped. ''I discharged this boy and he'll stay
discharged.''

With that retort the man turned and walked
away abruptly. Joe stared disconsolately after
him, looking as if he were about to cry again.

''Never mind,'' Louise said encouragingly.
''You'll find a better job.''

Joe shook his head. ''No one wants to hire
a fourteen-year-old kid. Wherever I apply for
work it's always the same. They say I should
be in school.''

''Where do you live?'' Jean asked abruptly.

''Clark Road. It's not far from here.''

The Dana girls exchanged questioning looks. Should they abandon their trip to the ice cream store and postpone the remainder of their shopping tour in order to visit the Doke family? It seemed to them the right thing to do. They quietly broached the matter to Evelyn, who was very willing to alter her plans for the day.

"We'd like to meet your mother and sisters," Louise told the boy. "May we go home with you?"

"Of course. Perhaps you can explain things to Mother—about the job, I mean."

"We'll do more than that," Jean promised.

At the first grocery store they passed the girls halted to purchase two large baskets of food. For the Dana girls this meant giving up new sports sweaters they had intended to buy that day. They did not really mind, however, for they liked helping those less fortunate than themselves.

"This is sure nice of you," Joe thanked them earnestly. "We haven't had good things like this for months. Celery! And real steak! Gee!"

The boy's spirits had improved greatly by the time the girls reached a shabby house on Clark Road, where the Dokes lived. The tiny yard, barren of grass because of large shade trees, was deserted.

"Belle and Daisy are usually playing out in

front," Joe explained, looking about him for a glimpse of his little sisters. "Maybe Ma took them and went somewhere."

The front door was locked but the rear one had been left slightly ajar. Joe flung it open, calling his mother's name. There was no response.

"She's not here," he began in disappointment, only to stop short. "Say, something's wrong! Ma always puts the house in good order before she goes anywhere."

The girls followed Joe into the kitchen. It was clean, but not orderly. A chair had been upset, and the contents of a cupboard were lying on the floor.

They hastened to the living room. There the disarray was even more noticeable. A rag rug had been turned up, papers were scattered everywhere, and the furniture was out of place. In one corner of the room a floor board had been pried loose. With a cry of alarm Joe rushed to the opening and thrust his hand down into it.

"Father's tin box!" he exclaimed. "It's gone! Stolen!"

The Dana girls were bewildered by the words —amazed that the Doke family should have anything worth stealing. It seemed to them that all good fortune had deserted Joe and his mother. They were deeply moved by sympathy for this unfortunate yet deserving family, but at the moment had no inkling that their interest was destined to lead them into an exciting mystery.

Through strange circumstances the Dana girls had become involved in many thrilling adventures, some at the school, some at home. Recently Louise had been mistaken for a fugitive from a women's reformatory. The resulting events drew the Dana girls into one of their most interesting mystery cases. The story of how they aided a talented young sculptress and her crippled charge is told in the story of the secret of the hermitage.

Evelyn Starr was the first to recover from Joe Doke's startling announcement that the tin box was missing.

"Did it contain anything of great value?" she questioned.

Joe's answer astonished them all. "I don't know," he admitted. "Mother and I never knew what it held."

"You never knew?" Jean echoed blankly.

"The box belonged to my father. He would not permit any of us to go near it when he was here. He made us promise that it should never be opened save in the event of his death."

"We must notify the police at once," Louise said. "If we act quickly the thief may be captured."

"I don't know what to do," Joe said uncertainly. "I think we should wait until my mother comes home."

"By that time it will be too late to do any good," Jean told him. "I agree with Louise that the authorities should be called immediately."

"Wait a minute!" Joe cried. "I think I see Mother coming down the road now!"

The boy had been standing within view of the living room window and had glimpsed a tall, thin woman with two children coming toward the house. He darted out and ran to meet them.

From the window Evelyn and the Dana girls witnessed a touching scene. They saw Joe talking excitedly, evidently relating the misfortunes which had occurred during her absence. Mrs. Doke seemed stunned by the news. She sank down on a doorstep near by and burst into tears.

"Poor thing!" Jean commented sympathetically. "So much bad news all at once is just more than she can bear."

"And she hasn't heard the worst part, if the injured pilot is her husband," Louise added. "Shall we tell her about that?"

"Maybe we should wait," Jean said doubtfully. "Such news will be a dreadful shock to her, especially after all this trouble."

"I wonder what the stolen box contained?" Louise mused. "If Mason Doke is a forger it may have held money obtained dishonestly."

"Or perhaps stolen bonds," Jean suggested. "I can't imagine anyone having a box in the house and not knowing what it held. I should want to find out what was in it."

Louise was on the verge of making a response when a queer expression came over her face.

"What was that?" she demanded.

The other girls had heard the same sound. They were instantly convinced that someone was hiding in an adjoining bedroom. With one accord the three ran in the direction of the noise. Louise jerked open the inner door. They were just in time to see a man with a black mask drop from one of the rear windows to the ground below.

"Stop, thief!" Jean screamed.

The masked figure did not halt. Clutching a small object under one arm, he ran around the north corner of the house and disappeared.

"He has the missing tin box!" Louise cried. "After him, girls! We can't let him get away!"

CHAPTER III

PECULIAR FOOTPRINTS

By the time the girls were outdoors there was no sign of the mysterious stranger.

"I saw him run around this corner to the right," Louise insisted. "And see! Here are his footprints in the soft earth!"

Jean had gone to the opposite corner of the building. "Why, I've found them over here, too!" she exclaimed. "The footprints half circle the house!"

"Then the thief hasn't gone far," Louise said grimly. "You go one way and I'll try the other."

The girls instantly separated, Evelyn and Louise following the trail to the right, Jean the one to the left. The latter, rounding the first corner at a run, collided full-force with her quarry.

Momentarily stunned by the unexpected encounter, the masked man staggered back a step. Jean made a wild grab for the tin box. She succeeded in striking it a firm blow which knocked it from the thief's hand.

The lid fell open and paper money scattered

19

over the ground. Both Jean and the masked thief made a dive for the container. They were struggling desperately when Evelyn and Louise came running around the house.

Realizing that he would prove no match for three athletically-inclined girls, the man turned and fled, abandoning the tin receptacle. He darted into the shrubbery and disappeared.

Evelyn raced after him, but very quickly gave up the chase. "That fellow runs like a track star," she complained. "He was out of sight before I even got started."

The Danas had realized that they could not hope to overtake the fleet housebreaker, so they turned their attention to the tin box. Evelyn found the girls gathering up the money which was being scattered by the wind. She hastened to aid her chums.

"Is it real, do you suppose?" she gasped in awe. "I never saw so many greenbacks before in all my life!"

"It's real enough," Louise answered, returning the last of the strewn bills to the container, "or at least I think it is. It doesn't have the appearance of counterfeit money."

Just at that moment Joe and his mother, followed by the two golden-haired children, came hurrying up. From a distance they had witnessed the chase but had been too far away to see all that had transpired.

"The tin box—did you get it back?" Mrs. Doke demanded breathlessly.

Then she saw that Louise was holding it out toward her. The lid was open, revealing the neat stacks of bills.

Mrs. Doke was too dumbfounded at what she saw to accept the receptacle. She gazed stupidly at it, then shook her head in a dazed sort of way.

"My husband left all that money? It does not seem possible. Mason never held a good job in his life."

"Shall we carry the box into the house before the neighbors become too interested?" Jean asked. "I think I see a woman next door peering out from behind a curtain."

"Yes, yes," Mrs. Doke murmured, "do come in."

When they were all inside the homestead Joe introduced each of the girls by name to his mother. Her manner as she thanked them for their kindness was distracted, however. Louise and Jean guessed that she was troubled regarding the contents of the tin box.

"I think we should notify the police to be on the lookout for the masked thief who broke into your house, Mrs. Doke," Louise suggested. "If you like, I'll go to the corner drug store and phone now."

"Oh, no, please don't! That is—wait. I

must have time to think this matter out. I
don't know what to do. I'm all upset.''

"The money will come in pretty nice, Ma,"
Joe declared with a grin. "It makes up for
me losing my job.''

Mrs. Doke gave her son a queer glance which
was not lost upon the girls. They wondered
what was passing through her mind. Louise
thought she knew why the woman did not seem
pleased over the discovery of the money.

"Mama, I'm hungry." The four-year old
Belle, pretty as a picture despite a state of
undernourishment, tugged at her mother's
skirt.

An expression of pain crossed Mrs. Doke's
lined face. She stooped and gathered the child
into her arms.

"Ma, there's lots of food in the house,"
Joe announced gaily. "Sacks and sacks of it.
See!''

He indicated the packages which Evelyn and
the Dana girls had brought with them. Tears
came into Mrs. Doke's eyes.

"You are so good," she murmured, "so
good.''

"We'll stay and help you tidy up the house,"
Jean offered quickly, embarrassed by the worshipful expression in the woman's eyes.
"Evelyn and I can do that while Louise helps
you prepare a meal for the children.''

"They've had only a few crusts of bread," Mrs. Doke admitted.

Jean and Evelyn soon had the house in order, and then helped Louise. Mrs. Doke was too nervous and upset to be of much assistance, although she tried hard to keep her mind on what she was doing. While the food was cooking Joe and the children lingered near, sniffing at the fragrant odors and begging for samples of what was being prepared.

At length everything was ready and they all sat down. Evelyn and the Dana girls made only a pretense at eating, for they had taken their usual midday meal at Starhurst. It warmed their hearts to see the children enjoy to the fullest the tasty food, but they were sorry that Mrs. Doke was too upset to partake of much.

While Evelyn and Louise washed the dishes, Mrs. Doke and Jean put the little girls to bed for a nap. Later, when Joe went outdoors to feed the scraps of food that were left to a pet hen which he was raising, Mrs. Doke broached the subject of the tin box.

"I didn't want to talk about it in front of my son or the babies," she said sadly. "They have no idea that their father—that is, I've tried to build up an ideal, and I'm afraid it isn't a true one."

She glanced appealingly at the girls, scarcely

expecting that they would understand, but the look of sympathy in their eyes encouraged her to continue.

"Mason always was a weakling. He had faults in his makeup which worried me half to death. When my husband told me about the tin box, warning me that I must never open it until his death, I was actually afraid. I hated the sight of it but I dared not touch it for I had given my promise not to. Until today I did not know what it contained."

"You need not blame yourself for the promise being broken," Jean said. "You couldn't help learning about the contents."

"It isn't the promise that worries me. Oh, I may as well say it right out—I'm afraid the money was stolen!"

If Mrs. Doke had expected her visitors to be shocked, she was mistaken. The three girls had arrived at a similar conclusion long before.

"Did your husband ever say anything to you which would lead you to such a belief?" Louise inquired.

"Oh, no! Never! But Mason kept things from me. He never told me about his business affairs. I need this money desperately, especially since Joe has lost his job, but I'd rather starve than use a penny of stolen money."

Mrs. Doke began to sob again. The girls shifted uneasily in their chairs, wishing that they could think of something comforting to say.

"Oh, if I could only locate my husband!" Mrs. Doke remarked after a time. "I would face him with more courage now. I'd force him to tell me where he found this money."

Louise started to speak, then firmly closed her lips. She was strongly tempted to tell Mrs. Doke that a man who might be her husband was aboard the *Balaska,* but knew that such a statement would bring out the entire story of the accident. The shock of learning that her husband was critically injured might prove too great for the frail woman. Louise reasoned that it would be wise to let word be received direct from the ship. It was possible that the newspaper reports had exaggerated the seriousness of Mason Doke's condition. In that event, by postponing the revelation Mrs. Doke might be spared such painful news.

Jean, however, could not resist giving the woman a slight hint of what had happened. "It's possible we may be able to help you locate your husband," she said quietly.

"You know where Mason is living?" Mrs. Doke asked eagerly. "How soon can you take me to him?"

"I am not sure that I can do that," Jean answered evasively, ignoring the first question.

The doorbell rang. Before Mrs. Doke could

answer it, the girls heard Joe talking with someone on the front porch. Their voices rose higher and higher.

"Dear me," Mrs. Doke said, moving hurriedly toward the door, "I hope Joe isn't quarreling with a peddler."

Evelyn and the Dana girls followed the woman to the front porch. Joe was engaged in a heated argument with a boy several years his senior. The latter was dressed in messenger uniform, and the girls correctly guessed that he was employed at the place where Joe had worked.

"So you lost your job, eh?" the older boy taunted. "Served you right. You always were a no-good loafer!"

"That's a lie!" Joe retorted furiously. "I worked a lot harder than you ever did. What business have you coming here, anyway?"

Insolently the other boy held up a telegram.

"You needn't think I'd come down this old dirty street if I didn't have official company business."

"Give me that telegram," Joe commanded.

"Oh, no, it's for your mother. Bad news too, I'll bet."

Mrs. Doke and the girls reached the doorway in time to hear the last remark.

"You have a telegram for me?" the woman faltered.

Assuming a more respectful manner, the messenger boy handed it to her. With trembling fingers she signed the receipt.

"Perhaps it is from Mason," she murmured.

Ripping open the envelope, she stared at the message. All color drained from her thin face, and then she began to sob hysterically.

"Oh! Oh! Tell me that it isn't true! Tell me that there's been some mistake!"

In her anguish Mrs. Doke thrust the telegram into Louise's hand. The girl read the message and glanced hopelessly at Jean. There was nothing either of them could say. The wire had been sent by none other than their own Uncle Ned, and contained the news from which they had hoped to shield Mrs. Doke.

The message read:

"Mason Doke critically injured in airplane crash on *Balaska*. Wire instructions."

CHAPTER IV

The Mysterious Stranger

"Don't you suppose it's a mistake?" Mrs. Doke murmured brokenly. "This can't mean my husband. Mason always wanted to take up flying, but to my knowledge he never did."

Evelyn Starr and the Dana girls longed to reassure the woman, but they knew that it would do no good to arouse any false hopes.

"You must be brave and strong, Mrs. Doke," Louise said gently.

"Then it's true? You've known it all the time. It is my husband who has been critically injured."

"Captain Dana is our uncle," Jean explained. "We learned today of the accident, and had hoped to spare you the distressing news until we were absolutely certain that the flier Mason Doke and your husband were the same person."

"There might be a mistake——"

"I am afraid not," Louise said, hating herself for destroying even this glimmer of hope. "You see, Uncle Ned couldn't have known your address, had your husband not given it to him with the request that he communicate with you.''

''I didn't think of that,'' Mrs. Doke said slowly. ''I can't seem to think logically today. So many dreadful things have happened. What shall I do?''

''Uncle Ned expects an answer to his message,'' Jean told her. ''If you like, Louise and I can wire him for more information. Then you'll know whether or not to meet the boat.''

''How kind of you! I'll be so grateful if you will. If I had more money I wouldn't even think twice about going. As it is—the children—they must come first in my thoughts.''

''Of course,'' Louise agreed quickly. ''Jean and I will send the message right away.'' She hesitated a moment, then said, ''Perhaps it's none of my affair, but what do you intend to do with the tin box?''

''I don't know. Put it under the floor boards again, I suppose.''

''If I were you I'd take it to a bank. That masked thief may return and might not be routed so easily another time.''

''I can't go to the bank now. I don't dare to leave the children alone in the house.''

''Would you trust us to take it for you?''

Mrs. Doke smiled at the absurdity of Louise's question.

''Do I trust you? How can you ask that

after all the fine things you have done for me?"

"We'll take Joe with us to help guard the money," Jean said.

"Will it cost very much to rent a safety deposit box?" Mrs. Doke inquired anxiously.

"Don't worry about that," Louise smiled. "We'll take care of everything."

The tin box was securely wrapped in coarse brown paper to make it look like any ordinary package. The girls then took leave of the woman, and accompanied by Joe they started for the nearest bank.

They felt rather nervous at first to be carrying so much money, but as no one paid them the slightest attention they soon felt at ease. When the bank was only a short distance away Jean observed two familiar figures walking down the street.

"Lettie Briggs and Ina Mason! What miserable luck to meet them!"

"Just speak, then walk right past," Louise advised in an undertone.

This the girls attempted to do, but Lettie, her eye drawn to the curious-shaped bundle, neatly blocked the sidewalk.

"Imagine meeting you here, and with your new friend, the telegraph boy!" she drawled. "Are you carrying a picnic lunch in that big package?"

"How did you guess?" Jean retorted, forcing the girl to make room for them to pass.

Lettie and Ina stared after the Dana girls and their companions, provoked that they had failed to learn the contents of the brown package.

"I wish I knew where they're going," Lettie muttered. "You can tell by the way they all act that they're up to something."

"They're going into that savings bank on the corner," Ina observed.

"What business can they have there?" Lettie speculated. "I wonder if it could have anything to do with the package they're carrying?"

"They acted secretive about it."

"Yes, they did, Ina."

While the two girls were talking, a strange man who had been standing near a drug store on the opposite side of the street crossed over to accost them.

"Did you see three girls enter that bank?" he demanded abruptly.

Lettie and Ina were startled at the question. They regarded the man blankly.

"Answer me!" he snapped. "Did you?"

"Why yes," Lettie replied, recovering her poise. "What of it?"

"Do you know the girls?"

"Of course I do. They come from my school."

"What are their names?"

Lettie did not like the harsh manner of the stranger, but she was afraid not to answer.

"Evelyn Starr and Louise and Jean Dana."

"The Dana girls, eh? I might have known ____"

"What was that?" Lettie asked alertly.

"Nothing."

Turning, the man walked swiftly toward a dirty coupe parked across the street. He got into it and drove away.

In the meantime the Dana girls and their companions, unaware that they were under discussion, entered the vestibule of the bank. Jean tried the door and found it locked.

"Oh, dear, the bank closes at four o'clock!" she exclaimed in dismay. "I had forgotten."

"Now what shall we do?" Evelyn asked. "It isn't safe to take the box back to the house, especially with that thief skulking about."

"Maybe another bank will be open," Joe suggested hopefully.

"They all close at the same hour," Louise said.

She regarded the brown package in deep perplexity. Then her face lighted.

"I know! Why not take the box to Starhurst? No one would ever think of searching for it there."

"I believe that would be the safest place,"

Jean agreed instantly. "Then, when the bank opens, we can transfer the money here."

Joe did not object to the plan. He would have approved of anything the Dana girls proposed, for by this time he was convinced that they were quite the nicest persons in all Penfield.

Lettie and Ina were loitering near the bank when the little party emerged from the vestibule. Although the Danas tried to ignore the pair, the Briggs girl and her chum refused to take the hint.

"I guess you forgot about the bank closing at four," Lettie began, hoping to draw them into conversation.

"Yes," Louise replied briefly.

"Were you taking that package there?"

"Since we had it with us, we couldn't very well *not* take it," Jean smiled.

"Someone was inquiring about you," Ina declared with an important air.

The Dana girls halted, for the first time interested in prolonging the conversation.

"One of my school friends, I imagine," Louise said carelessly.

Ina shook her head. "It was a strange man. He kept asking all sorts of questions about who you are."

"Can you describe him?" blond Jean asked quickly.

She realized that she had spoken in too eager a tone. Lettie nudged Ina, whereupon the latter immediately lost all desire to communicate any information.

"He was a tall man," she declared glibly. "Or let me see—was he short? I think he was dark, but he might have been light. He had brown eyes—no, they must have been blue."

Convinced that Ina was only attempting to make sport at their expense, the Dana girls and their friends walked away swiftly.

"Do you think anyone did ask about us?" Jean inquired doubtfully when they were some distance from the bank.

"Yes, Ina's voice had a sincere ring when she spoke of that man," Louise returned thoughtfully. "Of course, she is too mean to have given us any real information."

"I wonder if he could have been the masked thief?"

"I was thinking of that myself, Jean. Perhaps he followed us here."

"And saw us try to deposit the treasure in the bank."

"I'll feel relieved when we have the money in a safe place," Louise said, looking worried. "Let's call a taxi and drive directly to Starhurst."

"What about sending the telegram to Captain Dana?" Evelyn inquired.

"We can do that when we've looked after the treasure," Louise answered. "It frightens me to have so much money in my care."

Taking Joe with them, the girls entered a taxicab and soon arrived at the Starhurst dormitory. The lad waited in the hall while the girls carried the precious box to the Danas' room without being observed. Jean locked it in a lower bureau drawer.

"I don't relish leaving it here," she said uneasily.

"Nor do I," Louise agreed, "but if we keep the door to our room locked the box should be safe until we can shift it to a better hiding place."

Evelyn Starr had grown tired after such a strenuous day. She declined to return to Penfield with the Danas and Joe, so the three made the trip without her, stopping at the first telegraph office.

"I wish we could ask Uncle Ned to find out something about the tin box," Jean remarked as they prepared to file the message with an office clerk. "It would relieve Mrs. Doke's mind to know where her husband obtained the money."

"I don't see how we can incorporate that in the wire, Jean."

"No, we'll have to wait, I guess."

After the message had been sent, the Dana

girls took Joe home. He was very proud to be seen driving up in a taxi, and thanked them profusely for the long ride.

"There's one thing I'd like to do before we return to Starhurst," Louise said unexpectedly after Joe had disappeared inside the house. "It will take only a minute."

"What?"

"Measure the footprints of the robber. That information may come in useful later."

The Dana girls sprang from the cab and hurried to the rear of the Doke house. The half circle of footprints was still clearly visible. Using a piece of twine which she chanced to have in her pocket, Louise made a careful estimate.

"An unusually large shoe," she commented. "We can transfer this string measurement to inches when we reach Starhurst and find a ruler."

The Dana girls did not wish to have either Mrs. Doke or the neighbors observe their activities, so they hastened back to the waiting cab. A short time later they arrived at Starhurst.

At dinner that night Lettie and Ina made a point of asking prying questions, but Louise and Jean maintained a discreet silence. As the Dana girls were leaving the dining room, Mrs. Crandall approached them.

"I have a telegram for you," she said. "It came only a moment ago."

Jean accepted it eagerly, and thanked Mrs. Crandall for bringing it to the dining hall.

"Don't open it here," Louise warned her sister in an undertone. "Lettie and Ina are watching us."

The Dana girls hastened to their own room. They felt certain that the message was from Uncle Ned.

"I'm almost afraid to read it for fear Mason Doke's condition is worse," Jean said nervously as she ripped open the envelope. "Just think, if he should die without telling anyone about that tin box, the mystery connected with it might remain unsolved forever."

CHAPTER V

A Night of Adventure

The message from Captain Dana confirmed the Dana girls' fears regarding the condition of Mason Doke. The unfortunate flier had suffered a broken arm, a dislocated hip, and internal injuries which ·might prove fatal. Captain Dana had ordered full speed ahead for the *Balaska,* hoping to dock in New York early the following day, several hours in advance of his usual schedule.

"This news certainly won't be an aid to poor Mrs. Doke in her upset state of mind," Jean commented as she folded the paper and laid it away. "I feel so sorry for her. I wonder to whom her husband was signalling on the *Balaska* at the time of the crash?"

"I've wondered about that myself. Uncle Ned may know. We can ask him when he arrives."

Jean went over to the bureau. Unlocking the drawer she removed the tin box, which she placed on the study table.

"What are we to do with this? Have you any bright ideas?"

"Keep it here, I suppose—at least for the night."

"That's just what I don't want to do," Jean said quickly. "Has it occurred to you that we might have an unexpected visit from the masked stranger?"

Louise looked startled at such a suggestion. "He would never think of coming here, Jean."

"I don't feel too sure about that. Remember, some stranger talked with Lettie about us and undoubtedly learned that we stay here at Starhurst. Now, if that man should be the thief, he'd naturally conclude that we had brought the box here for safe-keeping."

"Maybe you're right. But what shall we do with the treasure?"

"We might turn it over to Professor and Mrs. Crandall."

Louise shook her head. "Mason Doke is Mrs. Crandall's nephew. If it should develop later that the money was stolen, it would create an awkward situation for the Crandalls."

"That's quite true. I hadn't thought of that particular angle. We'll have to do something with the box, though. I won't sleep a wink if we keep it here."

"You probably won't do much sleeping anyway," Louise laughed. "Tonight the Classical Club dance is to be held here at the dormitory."

"All the more reason why we should hide the box. Strangers will be roaming in and out of the building. Even if we do keep our door locked, someone might get in with a skeleton key."

"All right, we'll move the treasure to a safer place," Louise agreed. "You name the spot."

"Why not give it to the watchman to guard? He's perfectly honest."

"Not a bad idea," Louise approved. "If no girls are around, we'll do it now."

The halls proved to be deserted. With their precious cargo of money the Danas stole down the back stairway, past the huge kitchen, and out a rear door. Amanda, the fat colored cook, observed their secretive leave-taking. Noting the package which they carried she instantly jumped to the conclusion that the girls were up to another prank. She laughingly reported the incident to two maids in the kitchen.

Louise and Jean found the watchman working in the tool house. They were favorites of his, so they had no fear that he would refuse to grant them a request.

"Well, well, what are you up to now?" he demanded gruffly, eyeing the package. "Some trick, I'll warrant."

"We're here upon a serious mission this time," Louise responded gravely. "We should like you to guard this box for us."

"What's in it?" the watchman asked suspiciously.

Louise did not care to reveal the exact contents, so she said:

"Valuables belonging to a woman who lives in Penfield. We were to take the package to the bank for her, but we arrived there after it had closed."

"Leave it in the tool house if you like."

"Will it be perfectly safe?" Jean questioned anxiously.

"As safe as anywhere, I reckon. I keep the shack locked. When I make the rounds of the school property I pass here every half hour. I can keep a special watch over the place if you think it's necessary."

"The package is extremely valuable," Louise said impressively.

"I'll look after it for you," the guard assured her. "Here, I'll drop it down in this empty barrel and throw a gunny sack over the top. No thief would expect to find it in such an unlikely place."

The Dana girls returned to the dormitory, satisfied that the treasure would be protected for the night.

"I only hope he doesn't fail to lock the tool house," Jean commented uneasily as they hurried to their room to dress for the dance.

"If you start worrying about that we'll have

no fun at all tonight,'' Louise laughed. ''Forget that tin box until morning.''

She, too, might have felt nervous regarding their disposition of the Doke treasure had she suspected that at that very moment Amanda, the cook, was discussing the subject with a stranger who had called at the kitchen door.

''Yas suh, de Dana girls is students heah,'' Amanda admitted, in response to the man's question. ''Dey is lively as yearlin' colts, too— always a-tryin' to prank somebody. And if you asks me, they is up to no good right this minute. I just saw Miss Louise an' Miss Jean a pussy-footin' out de door totin' a square box!''

''Hid it somewhere, I'll venture,'' the man encouraged.

''I ain't sayin', but I did see 'em amble into de tool house with it an' talk to de watchman. But I don't try keepin' up with dem gals. Dey is too skittish for old Mandy.''

It suddenly occurred to the colored woman that she was talking entirely too much; yet even then she failed to realize that the stranger deliberately was seeking information. Announcing that she had work to do, she advised him to see Mrs. Crandall if he cared to learn more about the Dana girls. It disturbed her a trifle when the man walked away hurriedly without troubling to visit the front office.

By nine o'clock the Classical Club dance was

in full swing. It was entirely a "girl" affair. Since both Louise and Jean were excellent leaders they found themselves in constant demand. By eleven o'clock, however, they had begun to weary of the fun.

"I believe I'll go to my room," Louise suddenly remarked.

"Before we retire let's slip out to the tool house and make certain it's locked," Jean proposed. "I can't help worrying——"

"It was your idea to hide the money there."

"I know. I think the treasure is safe, but I'll sleep better if we take a look."

"All right," Louise said goodnaturedly.

They slipped quietly out by a side door. There was no moon, and the darkness covered their movements as it did also those of Lettie Briggs, who had chanced to observe the Dana girls leave the building. Determined to find out what they were doing, she stealthily trailed them across the lawn.

Louise and Jean went directly to the tool house. They were relieved to find it securely locked. The watchman, however, was nowhere in sight.

Suddenly a girl's terrified scream pierced the air.

"What was that?" Louise gasped.

"It sounded like Lettie Briggs's voice! The cry came from over by the lily pond."

The Dana girls ran in that direction. It was too dark for them to see very far ahead, but they could hear someone struggling in the shrubbery bordering the stream.

Jean was the first to reach the scene. She beheld the old watchman stretched out on the ground, apparently felled by a blow from a man who was struggling now with Lettie Briggs.

Jean sprang at the stranger, trying to force him to release Lettie. Her weight threw the pair off balance, causing them to sway backward toward the half-filled lily pond. Lettie screamed again, clutching at Jean. The three toppled with a huge splash into the shallow water.

Before Jean or Lettie could recover from the unexpected ducking, the man scrambled to his feet, muttered something under his breath, and darted away.

"Now see what you've done!" Lettie cried furiously, fishing a lily pad from her bedraggled hair. "Of all the stupid tricks! My dress is ruined."

"So is mine, Lettie. I'm terribly sorry. I didn't realize you were standing so close to the pond. I only wanted to save you from that man."

Louise had arrived by this time and helped the girls from the pool. She was less concerned with their plight than she was at that of the watchman, who looked somewhat dazed as he sat up.

"Are you hurt?" she inquired anxiously, helping him to arise.

"I'll be all right as soon as I get my breath. That scoundrel leaped on me from behind and tried to take my keys."

"He didn't get the one to the tool house?" Louise demanded quickly.

"No, he was struggling with me when that girl screamed. Then he knocked me down and turned on her."

"I would have captured him, too," Lettie interrupted, "if it hadn't been for Jean. Of all the silly tricks—pushing a person into the pond!"

"You were getting the worst of it when I ran up," Jean said shortly.

"I do hope the box of money is safe," Louise murmured anxiously without thinking to be cautious in her remarks.

"What money?" Lettie questioned alertly. Then, as no one answered, she added shrewdly, "Don't tell if you want to keep it a secret! But I can guess!"

"Let's see if we can find any trace of the prowler," Jean interposed hastily.

Borrowing the watchman's flashlight, the girls tramped about in the vicinity of the lily

pond, searching carefully among the shrubbery. To their dismay the man had disappeared. Suddenly Jean gave an elated cry.

"See this, Louise! His footprints!"

"And they run in a circle!" Louise exclaimed
in awe.

The Danas followed the trail, which they discovered led around the lily pond. The girls
were startled at their findings, for they tended
to confirm their belief that the stranger who
had attacked the watchman was the same man
who had entered the Doke home. Unquestion-
ably he had trailed them to Starhurst after
learning that the tin box was in their possession.

The circle of footprints was especially mysti-
fying even while it served to identify the
prowler. Why did the man always move in such
queer fashion? Louise reasoned that when
startled the stranger temporarily became confused, losing all sense of direction.

She bent down to measure one of the footprints. It seemed to be the exact size of those
she had noted earlier that day at the Doke
home.

Lettie Briggs was completely baffled by the
actions of the Dana girls. She hoped that they
would drop a few words inadvertently which
would give her some clue as to what they were
thinking. But Louise and Jean guarded their

speech. The former was provoked at herself for having revealed anything at all about the box of money.

At length Lettie, resigned to the fact that she could learn nothing more, abandoned the scene and returned to the dormitory to change her dress.

After she had gone, Jean, Louise and the watchman went directly to the tool house. To their relief the tin box was still safe in the barrel where it had been hidden.

Lettie, in the meantime, was enjoying the limelight. When a group of students gathered about her to ask what had happened she told a distorted tale, glorifying her own actions and belittling those of Jean.

"It would have served the Dana girls right if they had lost the treasure," she ended.

"Treasure?" Ina Mason demanded instantly.

"Oh, yes," Lettie said glibly, "that was what caused all the trouble—a thief came here to steal it."

"You're joking," one of the girls declared skeptically.

"It's the truth, and you may ask the watchman. He hid the box for them in the tool house. I'm not absolutely sure, but I think the treasure was sent here by Captain Dana. For all I know he may have stolen it from some passenger!"

After Lettie had gone to her room to change

her dress, the story spread rapidly. Soon one student was whispering to another that the Dana girls were harboring a stolen treasure which had been sent to them by Captain Dana. At first few credited the tale, but when others observed the watchman guarding the tool house, the story did not seem so preposterous. Captain Dana assumed the character of a pirate in the minds of many.

Jean and Louise noticed peculiar glances cast in their direction when they entered the dormitory. However, they went directly to their rooms and thus had no suspicion of the gossip which was circulating.

In the morning the girls did observe that something was amiss. They had no time to give the matter much thought, for shortly after breakfast they received a call from Mrs. Mason Doke. The troubled woman had spent a sleepless night worrying about the box of money and so had taken the early bus for Starhurst to learn if the treasure was safe. She seemed relieved when the Dana girls assured her that it was, yet even then she was not entirely satisfied.

"We plan to take it to a bank," Louise reminded her.

"I'm not sure that I care to do that, either," the woman replied. "The bank officials may ask embarrassing questions. I've been thinking the matter over. The best thing to do would be for me to take the box back to my home.''

"It will never be safe there,'' Jean insisted. "That masked thief is almost certain to pay you a return visit.''

"I don't believe he'll dare come back again.''

In vain did the Dana girls try to show Mrs. Doke that she was making a foolish mistake, but the woman remained adamant. Finally, convinced that they could not alter her decision, Louise and Jean offered to accompany her to her home.

"We'll help you hide the money,'' Louise promised.

A little later, while examining the Doke house from garret to cellar, the Dana girls discovered that a satisfactory hiding place for the treasure was not easy to find. At last, upon Mrs. Doke's suggestion, they decided to bury the box in the cellar.

Jean and Louise set to work with pickax and shovel. The ground was so hard that they were soon exhausted from their work.

"Let's try another place,'' Louise said. "How about that north corner?''

The earth seemed looser in the spot which she indicated. They had just begun to dig again when everyone was startled to hear a knock at the kitchen door. The Dana girls glanced in dismay toward the cellar window. Had anyone seen them at work?

"Quick! Hide the box in the fruit closet!" Jean directed.

While her sister moved the treasure out of sight, she went to answer the door. The caller was a tall, fairly well dressed man, his face half hidden beneath a drooping felt hat. He kept his head lowered as he muttered:

"Do you want to buy any pins or needles or safety pins?"

"No, thank you, I'm not buying anything to-day," Jean answered briefly.

She closed the door. Then she moved to the kitchen window and looked out. Some time elapsed before the man slowly walked away. Jean returned to the cellar, decidedly disturbed by the incident.

"The man was a peddler," she explained to Mrs. Doke. "At least, that was what he claimed to be. Somehow he didn't look like one and he carried no box of samples. Louise, you don't suppose he could have been that masked thief?"

Her sister did not answer the question, for she had become absorbed in a problem of her own. During Jean's absence she had resumed her digging activities. Now she was provoked because her pick had struck a hard object which refused to budge.

"It's a rock, I think!" she exclaimed. "Just our luck. That means we'll have to select still another place."

She gave the object an impatient kick with her foot and bent down to remove a little dirt so that she might view it to better advantage. She scraped away more earth. Then the pick fell from her hand and she uttered an astonished cry.

"Jean! Mrs. Doke! It isn't a rock at all! It's a chest! A buried chest!"

CHAPTER VI

The Buried Chest

Mrs. Doke did not share the elation of the Dana girls over the startling discovery. While Louise and Jean tugged at the heavy chest, trying to lift it from the hole, she stood nervously by, looking troubled.

"I wonder what it contains?" Jean asked in high excitement. "Perhaps more money!"

By this time they had scraped away enough earth to obtain a view of the top of the box. It was a heavy wooden container. Carved in crude letters on the tight-fitting lid were the words:

"Property of John Ely."

As Louise read the name aloud, Mrs. Doke became even more distressed.

"I've never heard of anyone by that name," she said. "I don't know how the object came to be here in the cellar! Do you believe me?"

"Why, of course!" Louise returned instantly. "I wonder if your husband——"

"Oh, I don't know! I don't know!" Mrs. Doke interrupted, wringing her hands. "I wish you hadn't found the thing. Cover it up quickly!

Never tell anyone that you found it. Please do this for me.''

The Dana girls gazed at each other and then at the chest. They were sorely tempted to lift the lid and learn what the contents were. However, they felt sorry for poor Mrs. Doke and could appreciate her feelings in the matter. It was obvious to them that the woman believed her husband had stolen a treasure which was hidden in the chest.

''Please cover up the box,'' Mrs. Doke pleaded as the girls hesitated. ''You both have been so good and kind. Do this for me, and I'll never forget.''

''It's for you to say,'' Louise responded in disappointment. ''The object is on your property. Of course, if you want us to bury it again that's what we'll do.''

''And you must never tell anyone about it,'' Mrs. Doke cautioned.

''We may as well bury the tin box with the chest since the hole has been dug,'' Jean suggested. ''That will save us another excavation job.''

Feeling decidedly crestfallen, the Dana girls transferred the box of money to the new location and then filled up the opening. They were just smoothing the earth and tapping it down with the shovel when Mrs. Doke heard a child's troubled cry from the floor above.

"Daisy needs me," she said. "I must go to her."

Jean and Louise finished their work before joining Mrs. Doke. After playing with the children a few minutes, they stated that they would have to leave. The woman accompanied them to the door, thanking them over and over again for their great kindness.

As Louise and Jean walked slowly toward the bus stop, they discussed the situation. It was not entirely to their liking. They wondered if they had done wrong in burying the chest.

"I shouldn't like to protect a criminal," Louise said soberly. "Mason Doke may not be one but it certainly seems strange that a box bearing another man's name should be found in his house."

"I wish we could talk to Aunt Harriet, Louise. She would know what to do."

"We might telephone her and ask her permission to come home for the week-end. She could easily arrange it with Mrs. Crandall."

The proposal appealed to Jean, so the girls entered a drug store to place their call. Shortly thereafter they heard their aunt's voice at the other end of the wire. Louise, serving as spokesman, explained that they wished to consult her upon an important and strictly private matter.

"By all means come home," Aunt Harriet urged them. "I will write a note to Mrs. Crandall without delay."

In due time arrangements were made at the school. Immediately after their last class on Friday afternoon Jean and Louise packed an overnight bag and departed for Oak Falls. Lettie Briggs, provoked because she had applied for a week-end leave of absence and had been refused, irritably watched them ride away. No sooner had they gone than she began a vengeful whispering campaign.

"Mark my words, the Dana girls expect to meet Captain Ned," she declared. "They probably intend to return the treasure to him before the police catch them hiding it!"

Actually, Louise and Jean were to be reunited with their uncle, but the pleasure was entirely unplanned. Captain Dana, upon reaching New York, learned that his schedule would permit a hasty trip home. Accordingly, he caught a fast train and arrived at Oak Falls scarcely an hour after his nieces did.

Jean and Louise were sampling a delicious apple pie which Aunt Harriet had baked especially for them, when the front door was flung open and they heard their uncle's hearty voice boom forth:

"Ahoy there! Anyone home?"

With cries of delight the girls hastened to the

living room. Uncle Ned, trim and youthful looking, gave them each a hug and a kiss.

"Well, well, this is a pleasant surprise, finding you home," he laughed. "That is, if you haven't been expelled!"

"Nothing like that," Louise smiled. "Oh, it's good to see you again, Uncle Ned. Did you wire Aunt Harriet you were coming?"

"No, I didn't have time. I suppose she's gone away for the day."

Jean shook her head. "She's upstairs binding Cora Appel's cut hand."

"What did that funny maid Applecore do this time?" Captain Dana inquired.

"Oh, she was dusting a lamp shade and tipped it over," Louise explained. "The bulbs inside the covering broke into a dozen pieces. Cora wasn't badly cut, but she's been carrying on dreadfully."

Harriet Dana, hearing her brother's voice, came hurrying down stairs to greet him.

"How happy I am that you were able to come," she cried joyfully. "I do hope you'll stay several days at least."

"I wish I could, Harriet. To an old sea dog this place looks like a bit of heaven. I've had a hectic voyage, to say the least. I'm very tired."

Captain Dana sank down in the easy chair which Louise offered him. It was then that the girls saw the weary lines in his face.

"Let me make you a cup of tea," Aunt Harriet urged, and then hastened to the kitchen before he could decline.

Louise and Jean did not ply Captain Dana with questions, for they knew that in due time he would tell them everything regarding the unfortunate accident on his ship. He sat quietly in a chair, his eyes closed and his body completely relaxed.

After fortifying himself with two cups of hot tea Captain Dana's spirits revived. He then gave a graphic report of the incident which had caused him such distress.

"I was not on the bridge at the time of the accident," he explained. "The first mate tells me that this man, Mason Doke, flew low over the ship, circling it three times. He seemed to be attempting to signal to a passenger who stood on the top deck."

"You mean that the salute apparently had been prearranged?" Louise questioned.

"Yes, the mate observed that the passenger, Briggs, had been waiting for nearly half an hour. Obviously he knew of Doke's intention to fly over the ship."

"Did you say Briggs?" Jean demanded in astonishment.

"Yes. The fellow was slightly injured when the plane crashed on deck."

"Why, he must be Lettie's father!" Louise

exclaimed. "What could he have in common with a man like Mason Doke?"

"That's what I'd like to know," Captain Dana returned with a touch of bitterness. "It's useless to question either of them. Doke seems to be a reckless, worthless—but there, I should say nothing against the poor fellow now."

"You mean—he's dead?" Aunt Harriet asked quietly.

"No, but I'm afraid he has only a few hours to live. At most a few days."

"How tragic for Mrs. Doke," Aunt Harriet murmured. Louise and Jean previously had given her a complete report of the facts they had gleaned regarding the Doke family. She likewise knew of their adventure with the treasure chest and appreciated the complications which would develop, should Mason Doke die without revealing why the box of money had been hidden in the house.

"I received a wire from Doke's wife only this morning," Captain Dana continued. "She is unable to make the trip to her husband's bedside. I guess she hasn't the money to buy a ticket."

"I am certain that is why she is not going," Louise agreed soberly. "She has every reason for wishing to see her husband."

"Where is Mason Doke now?" Aunt Harriet inquired thoughtfully.

"I sent him directly to the municipal hospital. The other injured passengers were able to go to their homes."

"Does Mrs. Doke realize how seriously her husband was injured?" Miss Dana asked quietly.

"I doubt that she does," Captain Dana answered. "I thought if I could spare a little time I'd drive to Penfield and talk to her."

"You're surely not thinking of returning to New York today?" his sister questioned in dismay.

"I must. We sail again at noon tomorrow. I shouldn't have made this trip at all, but I wanted to talk to you."

Captain Dana looked at his watch and hastily arose. "If I expect to reach Penfield I must start right away."

His sister pushed him gently back into the chair.

"Do sit still and relax for at least a few hours longer, Ned," she protested. "I'll save you the trip to Penfield by going myself with Louise and Jean. We'll talk to Mrs. Doke and break the news to her as gently as possible."

"That's good of you. Maybe that will be the best way, too. A woman knows how to handle a delicate situation better than a man does."

"Have you any particular message?"

"Only that her husband has been asking for

her almost hourly. If she wishes to see him alive she must make the trip to New York—and that very soon.''

"I'll urge her to go," Aunt Harriet promised.

All too soon Captain Dana was forced to say good-bye. Jean and Louise accompanied him to the railroad station. Upon their return to the house they found Aunt Harriet packing her suitcase.

"You must be looking forward to an extended visit at Penfield," Louise laughed.

"Perhaps I am," her aunt responded mysteriously. "I have a little plan."

"A plan?"

"You'll hear about it later."

Miss Dana refused to reveal anything further until she should have a talk with Mrs. Doke. Louise and Jean accompanied her in her auto to the house in Penfield, having no suspicion as to what was in their aunt's mind. As gently as possible the three explained to Mrs. Doke that her husband was in a critical condition.

"I don't know what to do," the woman said in distress. "I feel that I must see Mason, yet I can't bring myself to touch money which doesn't belong to me."

"I shall be glad to buy your ticket for you," Aunt Harriet told her kindly. "Do permit me to lend you money for the trip."

At first Mrs. Doke protested, saying that she

was afraid she might never be able to repay the sum.

"And there are the children to be considered. Joe isn't old enough to look after his sisters, and I have no one to care for them during my absence."

Aunt Harriet's eyes were shining. She was never so happy as when she could do a kind deed.

"I've thought of that," she smiled. "While you are away I'll stay here and keep house and care for the children!"

"So that was your plan, Aunt Harriet!" Jean cried. "What a splendid one!"

In the end the Danas convinced Mrs. Doke that nothing stood in her way of an immediate trip to New York. They helped her pack her bag and make final arrangements. When Louise and Jean returned to the house after driving the grateful woman to the railroad station they found Aunt Harriet well established in her new quarters. She had succeeded in making friends with Daisy and Belle, who gradually were becoming reconciled to their mother's absence.

"Everything will run smoothly in another hour," Aunt Harriet declared triumphantly.

"You certainly took upon yourself a man-sized job," Jean commented. "If only Louise and I could stay with you to help out——"

"Nonsense! The work is nothing. Of course, you'll both return to school."

"You'll be lonely here at night," Louise said, looking troubled.

"Not at all. I shall enjoy every minute of my stay. You and Jean must come to see me now and then."

"We'll do that whenever we can get away," Louise told her. "You may be sure of that."

The Dana girls deliberately refrained from speaking of the buried chest which had been hidden in the cellar, although the thought of it was uppermost in their minds. They were more worried than they cared to admit. They had a strange feeling, amounting almost to conviction, that during Mrs. Doke's absence the masked thief would pay a return visit to her house!

CHAPTER VII

A CLEVER DOG

"THE more I think about it, the more inclined I am to feel that Aunt Harriet shouldn't stay alone at the Doke cottage," Louise remarked to her sister as the two girls rode back to Starhurst School for Girls.

"I wish we could stay with her nights," Jean responded. "Why not ask Mrs. Crandall if we may?"

The proposal pleased Louise. Upon reaching the school the girls went directly to the headmistress's office and explained the situation to her. The requested permission was readily granted.

Just as they were leaving, the Dana girls encountered Evelyn Starr and paused to tell her of their plans. Lettie Briggs, who was loitering near by, chanced to overhear the conversation. She was especially irritable, because only a few minutes earlier Mrs. Crandall had refused her request to spend a few days in New York.

"It seems odd that some folks always have favors granted to them," she said with an angry toss of her head. "Especially persons who have no scruples about keeping other people's money."

"Now what did she mean by that remark?" Jean demanded when Lettie had hurried down the hall.

Evelyn hesitated, then said carelessly:

"Oh, there's a silly story going the rounds—something to the effect that you and Louise are guarding a treasure which your uncle stole from a passenger on his boat. It's ridiculous, of course."

"Why didn't you tell us before, Evelyn?" Louise asked.

"Oh, it was all so absurd. No one believes the story except a few of Lettie's friends."

"She probably started it herself," Jean said crossly.

"I'm sure she did."

"We have more important things on hand than the wild stories Lettie tells," Louise declared. "Usually her absurd tales strike back at her like a boomerang."

"I hope this one hits her with a good sound wallop!" Jean said grimly.

The girls separated, the two Danas going to their study room. In contrast to Lettie Briggs they both stood high in their work, and had no intention of permitting their studies to suffer, even though they were to be absent from school during a period usually devoted to lesson preparation.

After classes the Dana girls caught a bus which took them to Penfield. They left it several blocks from the Doke cottage and planned to walk the rest of the way. They had gone only a short distance when Jean called attention to a curly-haired brown dog which was following them. When they halted, it came up to them, wagging its tail and fairly begging to be petted.

"Isn't it cute?" Jean said with a laugh. "I wonder if it's lost?"

"It seems to be."

"I wish it belonged to me, Louise. I'd give it to Daisy and Belle as a present. They'd love the little fellow."

"It doesn't belong to you, so come on."

The girls continued down the street but the dog insisted upon trailing them. In vain did Jean sternly order it to go home. When they reached the Doke cottage the animal was still following at their heels.

"Whether or not we like it, we've acquired a stray dog," Louise chuckled. "If Aunt Harriet doesn't object I suppose it may as well stay until its owner shows up to claim it."

Joe, Daisy, and Belle, who were playing in the front yard, came running to meet the Dana girls. They asked eager questions about the dog, pleading so hard to keep the animal that

Aunt Harriet agreed it might remain at the cottage until claimed.

"His stubby tail keeps jumping up and down when I pet him," Daisy said in her childish lisp. "Let's call him Wags."

Wags took an immediate liking to his new home, displaying a mischievous streak which kept everyone busy. The dog had a mania for digging holes in the yard and around the shrubbery. When reprimanded he would look so innocent that no one would have the heart to punish him for what he had done.

Louise and Jean greatly assisted their aunt by taking entire charge of the children. They entertained Daisy and Belle by telling them stories and by building a doll's house. The latter venture was not entirely successful, however, for Jean pounded her thumb with a hammer, and the finished product had a decidedly lopsided appearance. Daisy and Belle, however, were delighted with their new toy.

Joe did not join wholeheartedly in the fun. The girls noted his gloomy expression and shrewdly guessed that he was fretting over the loss of his job.

"Cheer up, Joe," Louise said encouragingly. "You'll soon find another position."

"I tried three places this morning. No one wants a fourteen-year-old boy. I hear there's an opening for a clerk at Henderson's drug store down the street, but of course I wouldn't stand a chance.''

"I don't see why not," Jean returned.

"Mr. Henderson has always hired older boys.''

"Why don't you go down there and talk to him?" Louise urged. "It will do no harm, and you may convince him that you're just the person he needs.''

"If you think I'd have a chance——''

"You surely won't have unless you try," Jean said.

"We might walk along with you to the drug store," Louise added. "Perhaps we can help you by speaking to the man.''

Encouraged by their interest, Joe ran into the house to dress for the interview. He was soon ready.

"Don't be afraid to tell Mr. Henderson all about yourself," Louise advised as the three entered the drug store a few minutes later.

In the presence of the portly proprietor Joe was suddenly struck dumb. He did manage to stammer that he was looking for a job. Mr. Henderson studied the lad appraisingly, but shook his head.

"I need an experienced boy—a real hustler.''

"I'll work hard, sir. I'll do anything——''

"I'm sorry," Mr. Henderson interrupted. "You won't do.''

Louise stepped forward. She felt that Joe, because of his timidity, had not shown himself to the best advantage. Drawing the proprietor aside, she engaged him in a private conversation. At first the man seemed irritated at the girl's interference, but he gradually became interested in the difficulties which had been visited upon the Doke family.

"You say Joe is his mother's sole support?" he inquired.

"Yes, the family is dependent entirely upon his earnings. If you need a live, wide-awake boy you'll find no one better. Joe is honest and loyal."

Mr. Henderson hesitated, then said with a warm smile:

"Well, I'll give him a chance. I'll let him wait on the trade this evening. If he's satisfactory the job is his at twelve dollars a week."

"Oh, thank you, sir!" Joe cried gratefully. "I'm ready to start work now."

"No. Come around at eight o'clock. That will be soon enough."

Joe was so excited over his good fortune that he ran every step of the way home. He was deeply grateful to the Dana girls for helping him secure the position and seemed grimly determined to make good.

During the evening the Danas dropped in at the drug store for sodas; at least, that was their

excuse. They were highly pleased to observe
that Joe appeared to be having no trouble at all
in serving the customers. Mr. Henderson came
over to speak with the girls.

"You were right about that boy," he said to
Louise. "He's smart as a whip."

"Then you intend to keep him?"

"Yes indeed. He starts tomorrow on a regu-
lar salary."

At nine o'clock that night Joe went home, a
tired but happy boy. He tumbled into bed and
slept soundly until Aunt Harriet called him in
the morning. After breakfast the Dana girls
walked with him over to the drug store. They
wished him luck in his new work and then caught
the bus that took them to school.

Joe began his duties with a will. At first
he was kept very busy, but late in the afternoon
a slack period gave him an opportunity to chat
with the customers who lingered over their ice
cream. He was telling a high school youth
about Wags, the new dog, when a man of dark
complexion seated at the soda fountain glanced
up alertly. He listened to the conversation several minutes before he spoke.

"Say, I couldn't help hearing what you said
about that dog," he remarked. "Want to sell
him?"

"Why, I don't know," Joe stammered. "He
isn't really mine."

"You found him, didn't you?"

"Not exactly. The Dana girls brought him to our house."

"The Dana girls, eh?" the man echoed. A crafty expression passed over his face but Joe did not observe anything amiss, nor did he grow suspicious when the stranger adroitly questioned him regarding his home and family.

"See here," the man proposed, "it won't hurt to show me the dog at least. You don't need to sell him unless you like. How about taking me home with you when you're through work?"

"That won't be for nearly half an hour yet."

"I'll wait."

At four-thirty Joe was through for the day. The two then left the drug store together.

"You haven't told me your name," Joe reminded the stranger.

"My name? Peter Short."

"Do you live near here?"

"Well, not exactly." The man frowned at the question, and Joe did not feel like asking another.

The Dana girls had not yet arrived from school. Aunt Harriet was sitting on the front porch, busy with a basket of mending. Joe introduced his companion to her and then went to search for Wags, who had mysteriously vanished.

Peter Short was a glib talker and adept at

drawing forth information. Aunt Harriet, who was in a sociable mood, answered all of his questions good-naturedly, never dreaming that she was revealing too much.

Suddenly Wags came racing around the house with Joe in close pursuit. The dog darted down into the cellar. Peter Short sprang to his feet.

"I'll help you catch him, Joe!" he cried.

"No! No!" Aunt Harriet exclaimed involuntarily. "Don't go down there. Joe will bring him out."

The stranger paid not the slightest heed to her admonition. Before she could prevent him, he had moved to the cellar door and descended the stairs. Aunt Harriet hastily followed him.

"Wags is trying to dig another hole!" Joe cried. "He's found some loose dirt."

Aunt Harriet quaked inwardly. The mischievous dog had gone directly to the spot where the treasure chest was buried, and was throwing up a shower of dirt with his front paws, burrowing deeper and deeper.

"Joe, stop him! Don't let him do that!" she exclaimed frantically.

"We'll see what he's after!" Peter Short cried exultingly.

He dropped on one knee and began to throw out loose earth with his hands.

"Stop that!" Aunt Harriet ordered sharply.

She caught the man by the coat collar and tried to pull him away from the hole.

Peter Short whirled upon her savagely and gave her a push that sent her reeling back against the cellar wall.

"Keep out of this!" he warned harshly. "I'm going to learn what's hidden in this hole!"

CHAPTER VIII

THE SECRET CAVERN

AUNT Harriet was fairly beside herself for fear that the hidden boxes might be uncovered. Again she called out in protest against Peter Short's arrogant disregard of her command.

Louise and Jean, returning from school, heard her voice. Realizing that something was wrong they hastened to the cellar. Instantly divining that the stranger was trying to dig up the treasure, they seized him by the arms and pulled him roughly away from the hole.

"What are you doing?" Jean demanded sharply.

"Make him go away!" Aunt Harriet half sobbed.

"I was only trying to find what the dog was after," the man muttered.

"Leave this house and never come here again!" Louise commanded.

She thought the man intended to defy the order, but when the two girls moved as if to expel him forcibly, he reluctantly obeyed. Joe caught the troublesome little dog and carried it from the basement.

Wags squirmed and barked. The instant he was released he sprang at Peter Short, nipping the man's ankle. The intruder yelled in rage and pain, and kicked furiously at the animal.

"Wags, come here!" Jean called sternly, looking about for a stick.

A window flew open at the house next door and a woman looked out to see what had caused such a frightful commotion. People began to gather. Peter Short, more annoyed than he was hurt, took advantage of the resulting confusion by slipping away quietly. When Jean and Louise tried to find a trace of him later, they could not do so.

"I was very foolish to have had anything to do with that man," Aunt Harriet declared.

"He acted almost as if he knew what was buried in the cellar," Louise said with a troubled frown. "You don't suppose he could have been the fellow who came here before? The masked stranger?"

"Dear me, I hope not," Aunt Harriet shuddered.

"I thought he resembled him," Jean said.

"Whoever he is, he almost found the treasure," Aunt Harriet said nervously. "I'll not feel safe with it here in the cellar."

"It should be moved without delay," Louise offered as her opinion. "The bank would be the safest place for it."

Jean reminded her sister that Mrs. Doke had requested them not to take the money there.

"I know," Louise admitted, "but we must do something with it. After all, while she is away the whole responsibility for its safe-keeping falls upon us."

"I've just thought of a good hiding place!" Jean cried after a moment's silence.

"Where?"

"Do you remember the cave we found one day nearly a year ago when we were out hiking?"

"Why yes! We never fully explored it, either. It was in such an out-of-the-way spot."

"All the better for our purpose now."

"I believe you're right," Louise agreed. "No one would think of searching in that cave, and certainly not the masked thief."

The problem of carrying the two boxes to the selected hiding place was a matter requiring considerable thought. The Dana girls decided to wait until dusk before making the secret trip.

As soon as it began to grow dark they loaded the treasure into the rear compartment of their aunt's car and drove to within half a mile of the picturesque Elmo River. The spot was a desolate one, densely wooded, and with no houses for a considerable distance. The girls secreted their automobile in a clump of trees. Then, making certain that no one was about who might observe their movements, they unloaded their precious cargo.

"I know now how Captain Kidd must have felt when he buried his treasure," Louise chuckled. "I hope we can find that cave again without any trouble."

Jean was confident that she could lead her sister directly to it. They staggered along the river bank with their load, now and then sinking ankle deep in the soft mud. Frequently they were forced to rest.

"If it's much farther I'll give out before we get there!" Louise gasped. "One would think this chest was filled with rocks!"

"Perhaps it is," Jean giggled. "Why not take a look now and see?"

"No," Louise returned firmly, "we must not open the chest until Mrs. Doke gives us permission."

The girls trudged on with their burden. They would have grown discouraged, had it not been for the fact that now and then Jean noticed familiar landmarks which encouraged them to believe they were approaching the cave. Then they found themselves in a dense thicket not far from the river.

"I think this must be the place," Jean said, putting down her end of the chest. "Let's look about."

They parted the bushes but did not use their

flashlight lest the beam draw attention to their movements. Suddenly Jean gave a delighted cry:

"Yes, here is the mouth of the cave! Just as I remembered!"

Louise peered into the dark opening and shivered.

"We'll go in only a little way," Jean said quickly. "Some other time we can come back and explore the place completely."

Neither of the girls was enjoying the adventure, but they would not admit fear even to themselves. They joked and bantered as they dragged the treasure into the hole. Louise flashed her light about the limestone walls of the cavern.

"I wonder how far the cave extends, Jean?"

"Probably to the river, at least. I imagine the cavern was formed by the action of water. Listen!"

Far back in the tunnel they could hear the indistinct sound of trickling water. It seemed to come from a great distance.

The girls groped their way along the damp wall until they came to a branch-off passage. They followed it for a few yards, only to discover that it rapidly narrowed down to a niche which ended in a rocky inclosure.

"This is just the place to hide the treasure!" Louise cried jubilantly.

They went back for the chest and the box of money. Satisfied finally that they had disposed of the treasure wisely, they hurriedly quit the cavern.

"I wonder if we'll ever find the place again?" Louise asked doubtfully.

"I think I can remember the location."

"You might forget, Jean. Mrs. Doke would never forgive us if we should be unable to produce the chests."

"She might thank us for getting rid of them! But I agree that we must be sure we can retrace our steps here. We might do as did the pirates of old—draw up a map."

"Lettie thinks we're modern pirates anyway," Louise laughed.

Returning to the automobile, the girls found paper and pencil. Then, while the route was still fresh in their minds, they made a crude map showing the exact location of the treasure.

"Better make two maps while you're about it, Jean," Louise suggested. "We can each keep one."

When the girls reached the Doke cottage an hour later they found Aunt Harriet nervously awaiting their arrival.

"I was afraid some harm had befallen you," she said in relief. "I should never have permitted you to attempt such a dangerous mission alone."

"It wasn't dangerous," Jean returned lightly. "The treasure is safely hidden now and our worries are over."

The way things developed the following day indicated that the troubles for the Dana girls were only beginning. Louise and Jean, upon returning to Starhurst, sat for a time in the garden studying under the shade of a giant elm tree. Presently they arose and wandered toward the dormitory. When they reached the steps Jean halted sharply.

"My pocketbook, Louise! I left it on the bench."

"It must still be there. We haven't been away from the spot three minutes."

The Dana girls hurriedly retraced their steps, but to their dismay the purse was not on the seat.

"Are you certain you had it with you?" Louise asked. "When we came from Penfield you went to your room for a minute."

"So I did. Perhaps it's there."

The girls hastened away to search their living quarters. They did not observe Lettie Briggs and Ina Mason, who stood near by, hidden by the tall shrubbery. The two conspirators had picked up the missing bag with the deliberate intention of annoying Jean.

"It's a good joke and will teach her not to be so careless next time!" Lettie chuckled. "Now that she's gone, we'll put the pocketbook back on the bench.''

"When Jean finds it there later on she'll think her eyes have failed her!" Ina laughed.

Lettie, emerging from her hiding place, tossed the purse carelessly down on the stone bench. The catch snapped and the pocketbook opened, permitting the contents to scatter. Ina stooped to gather up the items.

"Oh, don't bother," Lettie said indifferently. But the next instant she bent down to pick up a folded paper which had fallen to the ground.

"It looks like a map!" Ina exclaimed as Lettie spread it out.

"That's just what it is, Ina! But a map of what?"

"Maybe a buried treasure."

The word "treasure" brought a sudden strange gleam to Lettie's eye. Abruptly she thrust the paper into the pocket of her sweater.

"What are you doing this afternoon, Ina?"

"Nothing."

"Then we'll go exploring together."

"What shall we explore?" Ina demanded. She had never been noted for her ability to think clearly or swiftly.

"Why, the trail indicated by this map, of course!" Lettie replied impatiently. "Unless I'm sadly mistaken, it will lead us to something interesting!"

CHAPTER IX

LETTIE'S INTERFERENCE

AFTER a fruitless search of their room Jean and Louise hastened again to the garden. There they met Evelyn Starr.

"Anything wrong?" she inquired. "You both look so worried."

"We are," Jean answered briefly. "I lost my pocketbook and it contained an important paper."

"The purse seemed to vanish into thin air," Louise added. "We were sitting by the stone bench——"

"Why, I saw Lettie and Ina standing there not three minutes ago," Evelyn interrupted. "They seemed excited over something. I didn't pay much attention."

"Lettie and Ina!" Jean echoed. "Now I'm beginning to understand."

The three girls walked quickly toward the bench. Ina and the Briggs girl had vanished, but even from a distance the missing pocketbook was visible.

"That's strange," Jean said in wonder. "It wasn't here a moment ago."

81

She caught up the purse and anxiously examined its contents.

"The map is gone, Louise!" she cried.

"You may be sure Lettie has it," her sister said angrily. "We must get it from her at once."

They searched the grounds and the dormitory. In vain did they inquire if anyone had seen either Ina or Lettie. If the two were at the school, most certainly they had gone into hiding.

"Oh, dear, what shall we do?" Jean cried, fairly beside herself with anxiety. "You know how prying Lettie can be. It would be just like her to sneak off and search for the treasure."

"We'll have to get to the cave first," Louise said grimly.

"But how can we? We have gym class to attend."

"We must skip it, that's all. The treasure is more important than half an hour of exercises."

Losing no time, the Dana girls slipped quietly from the dormitory. It took them nearly two hours to reach the vicinity of the cave, for they were compelled to walk the entire distance. They approached the opening of the cavern with extreme caution and were glad that they had, for they could hear the indistinct murmur of voices within.

"Lettie and her Ina!" Louise whispered. "They'll soon find the treasure."

Cautiously the Dana girls crept into the opening. They could hear Ina and Lettie talking together farther down the passageway. From their conversation they gathered that the hidden chest and box had not been discovered as yet.

"Maybe we can frighten them away," Jean proposed. "It's our only hope."

She began to make weird guttural sounds in her throat, not unlike those of a wild animal. Louise added to the effect by scratching with her finger nails on the rock wall. Then they rolled a few loose stones down the passageway.

At first the Dana girls feared their efforts were useless. Suddenly they were rewarded by hearing a muffled shriek. The next instant Lettie and Ina dashed into view and as quickly vanished through the cave door. Louise and Jean heard them crashing through the underbrush.

"They'll not come snooping around again in a hurry!" Louise chuckled. "I hope the treasure is safe."

After making certain that Ina and Lettie actually had left the vicinity, the Dana girls descended to the branch-off niche of the cave. The box and chest remained undisturbed.

"It will not be safe to leave the treasure here now that Lettie knows of the cave," Louise commented. "We'll have to move it again."

They set about transferring the boxes and

had just dragged them to the mouth of the cavern, when they heard someone approaching through the thicket. Before they could dodge back out of sight an elderly man with a fishing rod came into view.

Despite his years, the stranger walked briskly and with a youthful step. He noticed Louise and Jean huddling in the opening of the cave and laughed aloud because of their fright.

"Hello, there," he greeted genially. "Nice day for fishing."

"Yes, it is," Louise stammered. "We—we were just exploring this place."

"And maybe playing a little joke on your school friends," the man added with a chuckle. "I met them running down the trail, frightened half out of their wits! What is it? A sorority initiation?"

"Well, not exactly," Jean admitted truthfully. "But we were playing a joke."

"I thought so. I used to be quite a prankster myself when I was a boy. That was a long time ago. Later I became a teacher. One of my students had a queer kind of way of playing jokes. He had a talent for imitating handwriting, and thought it great fun when he wrote silly notes, signing other folks' names. Later it wasn't so funny."

"You mean the boy put his talent to dishonorable use?" Jean inquired curiously.

"Yes," the old man returned with a trace of sadness. "When he grew older he forged checks and various documents. He cheated many of his acquaintances and friends."

"I hope you did not lose anything," Louise said.

"Oh, I did. A thousand dollars. It was a bitter blow. The loss practically reduced me to poverty. But I'm not complaining about my lot. I have a comfortable cabin near by and I manage to get along all right. Today I wasn't so lucky, though. The fish wouldn't bite."

"You haven't told us your name," Jean reminded him, as she saw that the old man was about to move on.

"My name? Well, now, I didn't think you were interested. I'm Herman Waite."

After chatting a few minutes longer the man continued down the trail. Louise and Jean waited until his footsteps had died entirely away before they went back to their labors.

They dragged the box and chest from the cave. An intensive search revealed a rocky ledge near at hand which was completely hidden by overhanging bushes.

"This place should do for a few days," Jean said. "I doubt that anyone would ever think of looking here."

They carefully secreted the treasure and hastily left the vicinity. In walking down the trail Louise noticed a scrap of paper lying on the ground. It was the missing map. Evidently Lettie and Ina had dropped it in their flight.

The Dana girls had been so intent upon moving the treasure to a safe place that they had paid slight heed to the brambles and thorny weeds which choked the thicket. Now, as they emerged into the clearing they noticed that their arms were bleeding from scratches. Jean's dress had been torn.

"We look as if we'd been in a fight," she laughed. "I wonder what Aunt Harriet will say when we reach the cottage?"

It was nearly dark when they arrived at the Doke home. Miss Dana had been sitting on the front porch, watching and waiting.

"At last you're here!" she exclaimed in relief. "I've been dreadfully worried. I telephoned the school at five o'clock and Mrs. Crandall said you had left early in the afternoon. Where have you been?"

Louise gave a detailed account of the day's adventure at the cave.

"I'll be happy when this affair ends," Aunt Harriet murmured apprehensively. "I haven't enjoyed a good night's sleep since I heard about the treasure."

"Mrs. Doke will return soon," Jean comforted. "Our responsibility will end then."

Aunt Harriet arose from her chair.

"I'm glad you mentioned Mrs. Doke. I remember now that a letter came from her while you were away."

"What did she have to say?" Louise questioned eagerly.

"I don't know. The envelope was addressed to you. I'll get it."

The Dana girls followed their aunt into the house. They were hopeful that the letter bore encouraging news regarding Mr. Doke.

Louise opened the bulky letter, scanning the cramped handwriting. Her face became a study as she read it.

"Bad news?" Jean asked.

"Yes, the very worst," Louise answered soberly, handing her sister the letter.

CHAPTER X

A Startling Revelation

The communication from Mrs. Doke bore the news that her husband had died shortly after her arrival in New York. He was to be buried in the town of his birth, some distance from Penfield.

By checking the date on a calendar the Dana girls discovered that the funeral had been held that very day. Mrs. Doke was to return home on a night train.

"I must consult you immediately about a matter which deeply distresses me," the woman ended her letter. "I hope to right a grievous wrong, and trust that you and your sister will aid me."

"I wonder what she means by that?" Jean mused.

"I suspect her husband made a death-bed confession, perhaps in regard to the treasure," Louise answered thoughtfully. "We'll find out definitely tonight."

Although Mrs. Doke's train was not due to arrive until nearly midnight, Aunt Harriet gave Jean and Louise permission to meet it.

They were eagerly waiting when the woman, looking pale and wan, stepped from a day coach. She greeted the girls in a distraught way and had very little to say to them until they were riding toward the cottage.

"It has been a dreadful ordeal," she began. "But I am glad that things happened the way they did—had Mason lived he would have been a helpless cripple."

Jean and Louise were impatient to learn if Mrs. Doke had gleaned any facts regarding the chest which had been marked "Property of John Ely," but they said nothing, waiting for her to tell them of her own accord.

"I have a mission to perform now," Mrs. Doke announced. "I fear that I cannot accomplish it alone."

"We'll be very glad to help if we can," Louise offered.

"You have been more than kind. I do need your help. On his death-bed my husband confessed to a number of forgeries. The crimes preyed upon his mind. He wrote down the names of the persons he had defrauded and I promised that I would make every effort to see that they were repaid."

"Then the tin box of money which we found in your house was stolen?" Jean questioned.

"Yes, and the chest also contains money and several bonds. I hope there will be enough to reimburse everyone who was defrauded.''

''You spoke of a list of names,'' Jean mentioned. ''Have you it with you?''

From her purse Mrs. Doke removed a carefully folded paper. Louise stopped the automobile and switched on the interior light that they might examine it.

The list, written in a shaky hand, read:

Herman Waite...............due $1000.00
Barbara McKinley..........due $4000.00
Julia Bellington.............due $4000.00
Casey Riley.................due $3000.00
Jane Judson.................due $6000.00
Samuel Slayback............due $3000.00
Mrs. Mary Tito.............due $5000.00

''Why, that amounts to twenty-six thousand dollars,'' Louise calculated. ''That's a lot of money.''

''I'm afraid I'll never be able to repay it all,'' Mrs. Doke said anxiously. ''But I shall distribute every penny which my husband left me.''

''It may not be easy to find these people,'' Jean commented, frowning. ''There are no addresses.''

''I realize it will be hard. I thought you girls could help me trace the persons who should get the money. Perhaps it is too great a favor to ask of you, though.''

''We'll be only too glad to help you if we possibly can," Jean assured her quickly. "I was just wondering about the first name on the list."

"Herman Waite," Louise supplied. "Only today we met an old man by that name. Strangely, his conversation led us to believe that years ago he was defrauded by a man who might have been your husband. The amount stolen from him was exactly a thousand dollars, too."

"I hope he is the person," Jean said. "He needs money badly just now."

"I'll be glad to leave the distribution of the funds largely to you girls," Mrs. Doke offered. "However, we must act cautiously lest we give money to the wrong persons."

"I'm almost afraid of the responsibility," Louise replied slowly. "Perhaps if we all work together we can straighten out the muddle without making any serious mistakes."

After she had become acquainted with the facts in the case Aunt Harriet was willing to have the girls undertake the task.

"It will be an excellent test of your detective ability," she smiled. "If you succeed, you will have as a reward the satisfaction of knowing that you have performed not one good deed, but seven!"

That night the Dana girls lay awake until long after midnight, discussing ways and means of tracing down the seven unknown persons. Save for Herman Waite, they had no clue as to the whereabouts of any of Doke's victims.

"This will prove to be the most baffling case we've ever tackled," Louise declared. "But I like hard problems."

"Then I wish you'd explain how the masked thief figures in the affair."

"It's too much for me at the moment," Louise yawned. "The most puzzling part of all is the mysterious circle of footprints that man always leaves behind."

"I think about it most of the time. That's all the good it does, though."

"Let's try to go to sleep," Louise suggested drowsily. "Thank goodness, tomorrow is a school holiday. We can get up late."

Everyone breakfasted leisurely the next morning, experiencing a "let-down" feeling from the events of the week. A little after ten the Dana girls, accompanied by Mrs. Doke, set forth for the cave in the woods, there to recover the treasure which had been hidden in the thicket. Unknown to them, Lettie and Ina had visited the scene earlier in the day, making a careful examination of the cave.

"I don't believe we were frightened away by a wild animal," Lettie said when they failed to discover the treasure. "I think someone must have played a joke on us."

"If you hadn't lost the map we might have found the buried gold," Ina retorted. "The spot where the treasure was hidden was plainly marked with an "X." Now we can't remember where it was located."

"That's right," Lettie snapped. "Blame me! Who cares about the money, anyway? I'm sure I don't!"

The two girls thereupon returned to Starhurst, and for the remainder of that day would not speak to each other.

The Dana sisters and Mrs. Doke experienced no difficulty in finding the chest and box of money in the rocky ledge where it had been secreted. Louise readily convinced the woman that the only safe place for the treasure would be in a bank. She agreed that they might take it there.

First they carried the boxes to the Doke cottage, there to count the money. Upon unlocking the chest which bore John Ely's name they were elated to find that it contained many stacks of bills as well as government bonds.

The task of estimating the exact sum in the two boxes was more nerve-wracking than Louise and Jean had anticipated. Aunt Harriet and Mrs. Doke both assisted, but the latter's count did not always tally with the first check, which meant that the work had to be done a third time.

Soon the living room was cluttered with piles of money. The girls had never seen such large sums before in all their lives.

"'The king was in his counting house, counting up his money,'" Louise softly hummed as her nimble fingers sorted the bills.

"Oh, please stop singing!" Jean cried. "Now you've made me forget the sum I had in this pile."

The task continued, and at length it was completed. The figures when added up totaled a few dollars over thirty thousand.

"I never dreamed there was so much!" Mrs. Doke gasped. "It will be more than enough to pay all of those people."

"Of course we counted the money in both boxes," Louise replied thoughtfully. "The chest was marked 'Property of John Ely,' and his name does not appear on the list your husband gave you."

"I never thought of that," Mrs. Doke said, looking worried. "It may be that all of the money in the chest belongs to John Ely. In that case, it would be wrong to give his money to the others."

"Your husband did not mention Ely's name?" Miss Dana inquired.

"No, I intended to ask him, but at the end he was too weak to talk."

"Perhaps it would be wise to hold the money

until you know exactly how you wish to distribute it," Jean suggested.

"I should like to settle everything as quickly as possible. I feel guilty keeping the money even a day."

"Then you want Louise and me to begin our investigation of the people mentioned on the list?"

"Yes. Even at best it will take a long while to give out the money."

Directly after luncheon the entire treasure was transported to the bank, guarded by armed attendants furnished by the institution. Mrs. Doke heaved a sigh of relief when the cash was safely out of her hands.

"And now, since we still have half a day's holiday we may as well start our work," Louise suggested to her sister. "Let's try to trace Herman Waite."

The girls assumed that it would be a simple matter to locate him by finding his address either in the telephone book or the city directory. The name was not listed, however; nor did personal inquiry in the neighborhood of the Elmo River reveal anyone who had ever heard of the man. Aunt Harriet suggested that Mr. Waite might be traced through an advertisement in the newspaper, but Mrs. Doke instantly vetoed this idea.

"It might result in publicity," she protested.

"We must move quietly in this matter. No one shall ever know that my husband was a forger."

For three days Louise and Jean tried unsuccessfully to find a trace of the man, traveling many miles in the family car in search of him. Their school work began to suffer.

"I'm afraid we're destined to fail in our quest," Jean remarked gloomily one afternoon as the girls walked slowly toward the Doke cottage accompanied by Wags, who had become their faithful companion. "We know Herman Waite is somewhere in the community, yet no one seems to have heard of him. If only Mrs. Doke would allow us to advertise!"

Louise did not reply, for just then the dog darted down a side street, seemingly in pursuit of an old man who was walking slowly along with head bent low.

"Wags! Wags! Come right back here!" she called.

The dog did not obey.

"Perhaps he has found his old master," Jean commented.

They called again to the dog, then hastened after him. As they came up to the old man he turned toward them.

He was Herman Waite.

CHAPTER XI

A Bequest

While the Dana girls were overjoyed at finding the old man, they realized that he might not be the right Herman Waite. It would be best, they decided, to make no revelation about the money until they were absolutely sure.

After chatting for a moment about casual subjects, Louise adroitly brought up the matter of the forgery. At first Mr. Waite did not seem eager to discuss the painful subject, but gradually he grew more talkative until he finally added more details to his original story.

"Can you tell me the name of the man who defrauded you of your thousand dollars?" Louise urged.

"It was Doke. Mason Doke."

"Then you are the right person!" Jean exclaimed suddenly in elation.

"I don't know what you mean," the old man stammered.

"Of course you don't," Louise smiled. "I'm sure you think us very inquisitive and rude to pry into your private affairs. However, we have good reason for doing so."

"You are to receive your thousand dollars back," Jean added quickly.

"I—I don't understand. How can I get it back? It was stolen years ago. Even if I could trace Mason Doke I would have no money to hire lawyers. I scarcely earn enough to buy food."

The Dana girls then revealed the strange circumstances connected with Mason Doke's death, and Mrs. Doke's determination to repay all the people who had been defrauded by her husband. Herman Waite listened to the story in a sort of daze. They were forced to repeat the details several times before they could make him understand.

"This good fortune seems almost unbelievable," he murmured. "I'll soon be able to live like a human being again. I can buy new clothes—clean ones. And I can have good food to eat. You are sure there is no mistake? You would not play a joke on an old man?"

"The money will be delivered to you within a few days at the latest," Louise promised. "Possibly tomorrow. We will arrange a date for you to meet Mrs. Doke and receive the sum due you."

After taking down Mr. Waite's address, the girls hastened on toward the Doke home to report their success. The old man's profuse thanks had warmed their hearts.

"And just think," Jean said happily, "we'll bring joy to six other persons in the same way."

"I doubt if the money will do more good than in this case. Mr. Waite needs it very desperately. But I hope we'll be equally successful in our dealings with the others."

It was only natural that the Dana girls should be unable to pay as much attention to their studies as usual. They tried to concentrate on them, but it was very easy for them to allow their minds to wander. Fortunately they both stood high in their classes; yet once the instructor was compelled to reprimand Jean for day-dreaming.

Another time, Lettie Briggs overheard Louise whisper the name "Herman Waite" to her sister. She instantly jumped to the conclusion that the Dana girls had found a new boy friend. However, it gave her slight satisfaction to tease them about it for they laughed heartily at the idea.

Louise and Jean were too engrossed in their own problem to care what Lettie thought or said about them. They had selected another name on their list, that of Julia Bellington, and were bending all their efforts toward locating her. Thus far their only clue had been furnished by Mrs. Doke, who years before had known a family by that name. Several days were spent by Louise and Jean in tracing the Bellingtons, only to learn that there had never been anyone in the family by the name of Julia.

Refusing to be discouraged by their failure, the Dana girls selected the next name on the list. From Casey Riley three thousand dollars had been taken.

"The name seems strangely familiar to me," Louise mused. "I'm sure I've seen it in the papers."

"Perhaps it figured in some sports story," Jean suggested. "One might say it has a pugilistic sound!"

They devoted themselves faithfully to the sporting pages of all the newspapers, and even searched the files for many years back, but found no mention of anyone by the name of Casey Riley. Louise inquired about him from her gymnasium teacher, and as a last resort visited the managers of various papers. One afternoon her persistence was rewarded.

"Why, yes, I know a person by that name," the editor of the Penfield Post assured her.

"Where can I find him?"

It seemed to Louise that the man hesitated a long while before replying. Certainly he studied her curiously.

"The only Casey Riley of my acquaintance stays at the Red Lion Athletic Club. He's rather a rough sort of chap."

"Oh, that doesn't matter," Louise returned, and then blushed. "I wish to see him about an important business matter," she ended.

All the way home Louise kept thinking of the queer manner in which the editor had looked at her as she went out the door. Obviously he had thought it odd that she should wish to have any association with a man of Casey Riley's type.

"But what is his type?" Jean demanded bluntly when Louise repeated the conversation to her. "Actually, you didn't learn a thing against the fellow."

That night the girls wrote a carefully worded note to Casey Riley, requesting him to communicate with them at Starhurst School for Girls. They considered it wise not to invite the man to call until they knew more about him. It came as a distinct shock to them the following day when, as they were leaving English class, a maid announced that Casey Riley was waiting to see them in the parlor.

"But we didn't ask him to come here!" Jean exclaimed in annoyance.

"Well, since he made the trip we'll have to speak with him," Louise said.

"If I were you I'd not let Mrs. Crandall know you have a visitor," the maid remarked in a polite, yet critical, tone. "She doesn't care to have persons of—well, of a certain type come here."

"Gracious! What sort of character is he?" Jean gasped.

Despite the maid's warning, the girls were unprepared for their meeting with Casey Riley. As they approached the doorway, knowing full well that some of their curious classmates were loitering in the hall eager to glimpse the visitor, they heard a loud, quarrelsome voice saying:

"Put me out, will you? Just try it, you puny old man! You'll find yourself stretched out cold before you can say 'Jack Robinson.' I guess you don't know you're flirting with dynamite or you wouldn't make passes at Casey Riley!"

Jean turned as if to retreat down the hall, but Louise caught her by the wrist.

"We'll have to see this through now. Come on."

They entered the reception room. The newcomer, a burly man of nearly two hundred pounds, dressed in flashy sports attire, was still engaged in a heated verbal battle with the janitor. The girls did not know what the argument was about nor did they care. They were only interested in bringing it to an end before either Professor or Mrs. Crandall should arrive upon the scene.

As it was, they were too late. Before they could speak, the east door of the parlor opened and Professor Crandall entered.

"What is the cause of all this commotion?" he inquired stiffly. "Sir, if you have come to see me, I must ask you——"

"Don't bother to ask me anything, brother," Casey Riley cut in crudely. "I didn't come here to chew the fat with any old fossil like you. I came to see a couple of dames—girls to you."

Professor Crandall held his breath and his face grew red. Never in all his career as an educator had he been so disrespectfully addressed.

"Sir, leave this building at once!" he ordered. "We allow no visitors such as yourself at this school. Go at once!"

Riley laughed scornfully.

"Listen to the little fellow give orders! Take a look at my muscle and you won't make such a loud noise, brother."

"Oh, please do as Professor Crandall requests," Louise pleaded frantically. "Go out into the garden. We will talk to you there."

"Is this person *your* guest, Louise?" Professor Crandall asked in a shocked voice.

"He came here to see us regarding a strictly business matter. We have never met this Mr. Riley before."

"I trust not."

"I'm dreadfully sorry," Louise apologized. "May we come to your office later and explain matters?"

"Yes, I shall expect you."

Professor Crandall had softened somewhat, for the Dana girls were favorites of his. However, as they hastily ushered their unwelcome guest into the garden the educator frowned in bewilderment. He could not understand why Jean and Louise should wish to have anything to do with a coarse character of Mr. Riley's type. He wondered if he had done right in permitting the man to remain upon the grounds.

"Well, sister, what's on your mind?" Casey Riley demanded of Louise when the three were outside the building.

"We want to talk to you about a money matter. It concerns a man by the name of Mason Doke."

"Never heard of him."

"Then you're not the person we're after," Jean said in relief. "We can't give you the three thousand dollars after all."

"What's that?" bold Casey Riley demanded alertly. "Did I say I never heard of a man by the name of Doke? That's a good one on me. Sure, I know him."

"Mason Doke is dead," Louise said gravely.

"Now, I'm sorry to hear that. A swell fellow if I ever met one."

"Obviously you're not the Casey Riley from whom he stole three thousand dollars," Jean commented severely.

The expression upon the man's face altered swiftly.

"Sure I am," he maintained firmly. "But the poor fellow needed the money. I hated to lose that three thousand, but I never bore Doke any grudge because he cheated me out of it."

"You must have a charitable disposition," Louise replied.

She drew Jean aside for a private consultation. The girls were most unfavorably impressed with Mr. Riley, and doubted that he had ever heard of Mason Doke, despite his claim to the contrary. However, they could not allow their personal prejudices to enter into the matter. They must give him every opportunity to prove his claim to the money.

"We might take him to see Mrs. Doke," Jean suggested. "At least that will be an excuse for getting him away from here."

Casey Riley was very willing to accompany them to the Doke cottage. Louise and Jean were ashamed to be seen with the man, and knew that both Aunt Harriet and Mrs. Crandall would disapprove. However, they felt they would be safe on a bus, so took that method of transportation. Fortunately the ride would not be long. As they left the school grounds they were painfully aware that many of their schoolmates had gathered to witness the departure.

During the ride Casey Riley skillfully tried

to draw information from the Dana girls. They revealed very little and consequently were dismayed at his shrewd guesses. They began to fear that they had involved themselves with a sharp crook.

Almost apologetically Louise introduced the man to Mrs. Doke. She had no opportunity of warning the woman to be cautious in her speech. In a few minutes of conversation the widow had made the entire situation clear to her unscrupulous visitor.

"I'm the Casey Riley you're looking for," the man declared. "Just hand over the three thousand and we'll forget about it."

"But I'm not sure—" Mrs. Doke began.

He cut her off rudely. "You heard what I said. I'm a man of few words and quick action. Give me that money now, or else——"

"Or else what?" Louise interposed coldly. "We'll not tolerate any of your cheap threats."

"You keep out of this, sister!"

"Oh, let's turn the money over to him and be done with it," the poor woman cried nervously. "Then he will go."

"Sure, give me the three thousand and I'll leave."

"I'd never pay this man until you have absolute proof of his identity," Jean cautioned.

"He is an impostor," Louise added firmly.

"An impostor, am I?" Casey Riley shouted

furiously. "You'll give me that money or I'll take it by force!"

Seizing a chair, he hurled it against the wall. It splintered into several pieces. Mrs. Doke screamed in terror.

"Turn off your siren or I'll break every stick of furniture in the place!" the man growled. "You've only seen a sample of what I can do. Now haul out that money before I lose my temper!"

CHAPTER XII

A Troublesome Caller

Unobserved by Casey Riley, Jean had slipped quietly out the side door to summon aid. She cried frantically for help. Chance favored her. At the next road intersection a police car could be seen slowly cruising along.

Again Jean screamed and waved. Her cries were heard by the alert officers. The car turned and came at full speed toward the Doke cottage.

Jean did not need to explain what was wrong. Even from the street one could hear the infuriated Riley breaking up the furniture.

The officers rushed into the house, grasping the culprit firmly by the arms. As he struggled to free himself, they snapped steel cuffs over his wrists.

"Well, well, if it isn't our old friend Jim Murphy," one of the policemen said jovially. "Seems like old times to find you at work again."

"Is this man known to the police?" Louise questioned.

"Very well indeed, Miss. He is a notorious

swindler. We've been on the watch for him over a year now.''

"He claimed to be Casey Riley."

"That's his latest alias, Miss. He's a violent customer when crossed. What was his little game this time?''

Without revealing anything which would prove embarrassing to Mrs. Doke, the Dana girls explained how they had come in contact with Murphy.

"You say you're looking for a man named Casey Riley?" one of the policemen inquired with interest. "Say, I know a person who answers to that title. He's not a crook, either!''

"An athlete?" Jean inquired skeptically.

"This man is an invalid. He lives in a beautiful home at some resort place. Let me see, I'm pretty sure it's Lake Acquila.''

The girls tried to learn more, but the policeman had told all he knew. Soon Jim Murphy was led away and the Doke cottage became tranquil.

"We must go to Lake Acquila at the first opportunity,'' Louise declared as she and Jean discussed their latest clue.

"It may prove another dead-end lead.''

"Yes, but if we're to succeed the only way is to trace down every clue.''

Aunt Harriet did not favor allowing the girls to make the trip to Lake Acquila alone, so after some hesitation she agreed to accompany them. The following week-end found the three entrained for the resort city.

They were directed to a beautiful estate bordering the lake. A maid ushered them into a comfortable den lined with tall shelves of books. Near the window in a wheel chair sat a middle-aged, kindly-faced gentleman, who greeted the Danas cordially, making them feel entirely at their ease.

In launching into their story Louise and Jean were careful not to reveal too much, for their experience with Jim Murphy had taught them a severe lesson. However, the mere mention of Mason Doke's name was all that was necessary. Casey Riley took up the story and his words carried conviction. He explained that years before the swindler had robbed him in a business deal by forging a check for three thousand dollars.

"Fortunately, I was able to stand the loss," he finished his story. "I always intended to trace the man, but my health has been poor. For three years now I have not taken a step from my wheel chair. The doctors thought it best for my peace of mind that I forget the entire matter. I have not been able to do that."

It gave Jean and Louise genuine happiness to reveal Mrs. Doke's wish that her husband's debt be paid in full.

"This is indeed an unexpected windfall," he smiled. "One good turn deserves another. I shall reward you both for adjusting this matter in my favor."

"Oh, no," the Dana girls protested firmly, "we could not accept a reward."

"Then I shall give the money to charity. My income is sufficient for my needs. If I were able to buy a new back—but then, I must not complain."

The hour had grown late, for Aunt Harriet and the girls lingered far longer than they had intended. Jean glanced in dismay at the clock.

"Why, it's nearly four o'clock," she cried, "and our train leaves exactly on the hour."

"Then you will never make it," Mr. Riley said, taking out his watch. "It is three minutes to four now. That clock is always slow."

"When does the next eastbound train leave?" Miss Dana inquired anxiously.

"Not until tomorrow morning."

"Then we shall have to spend the night at a hotel."

"Not unless you choose to," Mr. Riley smiled. "I should like nothing better than to have you stay here as my guests. I have ten empty bedrooms. You will do me a great favor by remaining, for I am a very lonely man."

Aunt Harriet graciously accepted the kind invitation. Jean and Louise were delighted at an opportunity to stay over night at the estate. Best of all, it gave them a chance to become better acquainted with their charming host.

The girls were shown to luxurious quarters, each room having a bath attached. Later they wandered about the grounds and sat with Mr. Riley on the veranda which overlooked the blue lake.

"You are a very fortunate man to own such a wonderful estate," Jean remarked dreamily. "I could sit here forever just gazing out over the water."

"You say that, my child, because you have never known what punishment it can be—just to sit and sit. For years I have been chained to this chair. The doctors can do nothing for me."

Louise and Jean tried to express their sympathy. Presently their gay manner and youthful talk returned. This gradually had a cheering effect upon Mr. Riley, and soon he was laughing at one of Jean's sallies. Just then a male servant appeared.

"I beg your pardon, sir, but it is time for your medicine."

"Medicine! It never did me any good. These girls are the best tonic I've had in years."

"Sorry, sir," the servant said stiffly, "but the doctor's orders are that you are to take the pills every hour. And you were warned, sir, that you must have no excitement." As he spoke, the man stared coldly at Louise and Jean, implying by his look that their presence was having a harmful influence.

"Oh, well, I suppose I'll have to do it," Mr. Riley complained. "You may wheel me into the house, Jennings."

"Jennings hasn't taken much of a fancy to us," Jean smiled when she and Louise were alone.

"No, I guess he thinks we'll make poor Mr. Riley worse. He needs someone to cheer him up."

"I wish we really could do something to help him, Louise. Money means nothing in his case."

"I fear there is very little we can do," Louise sighed.

Aunt Harriet and her nieces retired early that evening after enjoying an excellent dinner with Mr. Riley in the spacious dining room.

"I shall sit up for a time," their host explained. "Doctor Kilman expects to drop in during the evening for a professional visit."

Louise and Jean were indulging in the luxurious pastime of reading in bed when they heard the doctor's voice in the hallway. It was then ten o'clock. At eleven he left the house, or at least the Dana girls assumed such to be the case, for his loud voice boomed a hearty "good night," and immediately thereafter a downstairs door slammed.

The Dana girls snapped off their light, intending to go to sleep. Jean arose to open the French windows. Moonlight flooded into the darkened room and she stood for a moment viewing the splendor of the garden. Unexpectedly the voice of Doctor Kilman reached her ears, though he was speaking in a soft tone which was almost a whisper.

"If we manage this thing right, Jennings, there's a tidy sum in it for both of us. It's not to my advantage to have Mr. Riley get well too soon. I haven't told him the real cause of his trouble—pressure on the spine. He thinks he will always be a hopeless cripple and we'll let him go on thinking that for a time."

"While we collect fat fees, eh?" the servant chuckled.

"That's it exactly," the doctor replied. "Whatever I collect, and it will be plenty, I will split fifty-fifty with you. Your job will be to make sure that Riley doesn't get wise."

"Trust me for that, sir."

Jean was aghast at the conversation she had overheard. As she crouched by the window, Doctor Kilman and the servant emerged from a small porch directly under the bedroom. They gravely shook hands and separated.

"Louise, did you hear that?" Jean gasped, turning toward her sister.

"Every word. How could any man who calls himself a doctor stoop to such a low trick?"

"We must tell Mr. Riley in the morning."

"Yes, of course," Louise agreed, "but he may not believe us. It sounds fantastic."

Oddly enough, Mr. Riley did credit the story when he heard it the following morning. He listened in stunned silence, then nodded his head.

"I have never trusted Jennings since the day I employed him," he confessed. "As for Doctor Kilman, I had begun to fear that he was a quack. Now I shall make a thorough investigation, thanks to your valuable tip."

Mr. Riley called Jennings to the den, and after forcing him to admit the truth he curtly dismissed the man from his service. He then wrote a letter to the state medical authorities, calling to their attention Doctor Kilman's unethical actions.

Louise and Jean assumed that the matter was settled. They were in their rooms gathering together their belongings in preparation for departure, when they were startled to hear the angry voice of Jennings in the upstairs hallway.

"You're not giving me a fair deal, Mr. Riley," he protested. "Please let me have my job back. I didn't know I was doing wrong in agreeing to Doctor Kilman's proposal.''

"I don't care to discuss it, Jennings," the invalid returned wearily. "Pack your bag and go."

Louise, alarmed by the servant's belligerent tone, had stepped to the bedroom door to peer down the hall. She observed her host seated in his wheel chair not far from the top of the stairway. The discharged attendant stood directly behind him.

Fear suddenly clutched at Louise's heart. Intuition warned her that Jennings, in retaliation for his dismissal, intended to do a horrible thing. She could read the sinister thought in his face. He was going to push the wheel chair down the stairs!

CHAPTER XIII

A Cruel Act

Just as the servant grasped his master's wheel chair, Louise screamed and darted down the hall. But she was too late to save Mr. Riley.

The invalid's vehicle rolled smoothly forward a few feet. The terrified cripple was too dazed to utter a sound. Then the wheel chair pitched downward, catapulting Mr. Riley head foremost to the very bottom of the stairs. He struck heavily and lay in a motionless, crumpled heap.

Jennings, horrified by his cruel act, turned, ran down a back stairway, and fled in panic from the house. No one tried to stop him.

Louise, calling for help, hurried down to the prostrate form. After that she had only a vague recollection of what happened, for doors opened, servants came running, and everyone talked at once. Mr. Riley was carried upstairs, a Doctor Smith was summoned, a nurse arrived. The unpleasant odor of ether issued from the closed bedroom. At last the physician emerged to face those who anxiously awaited his verdict.

"Mr. Riley will live," he reported quietly. "In a day or two he will be walking again."

"Walking?" Jean gasped, wondering if she had heard correctly.

"Yes, his affliction has never been as serious as he was led to believe by Doctor Kilman. Incidentally, that man had no right to call himself a doctor, for his license was taken from him years ago."

"That doesn't surprise me in the least," Louise commented.

"Mr. Riley has suffered from a pressure on the spine," the doctor continued. "Actually, the fall proved a blessing, for the nerve impingement has now been removed. Of course, Mr. Riley must have complete rest and quiet for many weeks."

"A sea voyage might be beneficial," Aunt Harriet said musingly.

"That would be the best kind of treatment."

"Perhaps we can arrange passage for Mr. Riley on the *Balaska!*" Jean suggested. "Uncle Ned would see to it that he received the best of care."

Later the plan was proposed to Mr. Riley, and it met with his wholehearted approval. The Dana girls then talked to their uncle by long distance telephone and made the necessary arrangements.

Louise and Jean were reluctant to leave Lake

Acquila, but their school work could not be neglected. When they went to Mr. Riley's room to say good-bye, tears of gratitude came into the invalid's eyes. He thanked the girls over and over for the happiness they had brought to him.

"I hope you will be able to bring the same joy to the others on your list," he smiled.

"We'll consider ourselves fortunate if we can locate even a few of the people," Louise replied. "It appears that we may never be able to find a woman named Julia Bellington."

"Julia Bellington?" the invalid repeated softly. "I once knew a young lady by that name. I would have married her, but I was stricken with this affliction."

Jean and Louise, excited by the information, began to ask eager questions. Their host was more than willing to tell them all he knew, though in recent years he had lost track of the woman. He promised to make every effort to trace her, that she might receive the four thousand dollars which was due her.

Arriving late in Penfield, the Dana girls went directly to Starhurst. Before they had had time to change their clothes a maid came to tell them that they were wanted in Professor Crandall's office. The summons was not wholly unexpected, for the girls knew they had a great deal to explain. They felt no misgivings, however, since Aunt Harriet had fortified them with a letter which explained their long absence from school.

Both Professor and Mrs. Crandall were waiting when Louise and Jean entered the office. The girls gave them Aunt Harriet's letter at once, and Mrs. Crandall read it carefully.

"Of course, your absence from school will be excused," she assured them. "Mrs. Doke telephoned yesterday to say that you would not return for some time, so we did not worry. Professor Crandall and I have called you here about another matter."

"Casey Riley—?" Louise asked, flushing.

"No, we understand about that too, for the whole story came out in the papers. We are proud that you and your sister had a part in bringing about the capture of such a notorious crook."

"We called you here to ask about Mason Doke," Professor Crandall interposed. "We understand that he died."

"I should like to learn all the details," Mrs. Crandall said. "I did not know my nephew well, but naturally I am deeply distressed over the tragedy of his unexpected death."

"Why not talk with Mrs. Doke?" Louise suggested.

"She does not know that I am her husband's aunt," the headmistress replied.

"Jean and I will be glad to take you there," offered Louise, who was reluctant to tell what she knew about the aviator.

An hour later the four arrived at the house in Penfield. At first inclined to be reticent, Mrs. Doke soon responded to Mrs. Crandall's kindly sympathy, and told the visitor the true facts regarding the property which her husband had left for distribution. Mrs. Crandall was exceedingly embarrassed by the disclosure of her relative's shortcomings.

At last Mrs. Doke spoke gratefully of the aid which Louise and Jean had given her. Professor and Mrs. Crandall were amazed to learn of the Dana girls' work and praised them warmly. They assured Jean and Louise that they might be excused from classes whenever an urgent need might arise.

"We know that you will not abuse the privilege," Mrs. Crandall smiled.

Since Mrs. Doke had spoken so frankly about her private affairs, the Dana girls felt no hesitancy in mentioning the various problems which confronted them in connection with the distribution of the money.

"There is one thing which really worries me," Louise confessed. "The name of John Ely does not appear on our list, yet the chest was marked as being his property."

"That does seem strange," Professor Crandall agreed. "Mason never spoke of the man?"

"Never," Mrs. Doke answered.

"Possibly the money was merely placed in a box which chanced to bear his name," Mrs. Crandall suggested thoughtfully.

"That is what we hope, of course," said Jean. "However, it would make an awkward situation, to say the least, should Mr. Ely lay claim to the money after it has all been distributed."

"I imagine you will never hear from him," Professor Crandall remarked.

A few minutes later he and his wife arose to depart. Just at that moment the doorbell rang, and little Daisy hurried to answer it. The child was gone for some time. When she returned she handed a folded note to her mother.

"The boy's waiting, Muvver," she said.

Excusing herself, Mrs. Doke unfolded the paper. She stared at it, then sank weakly into the nearest chair.

"Oh, dear," she wailed, "our worst fears are confirmed. This message is from John Ely!"

CHAPTER XIV

AN UNWELCOME MESSAGE

WITH a gesture of despair Mrs. Doke handed the note to the others to read. It was brief and business-like.

"Some days ago a chest of money was found in your basement. I understand it has since been transferred to a bank. This property is legally mine. I shall expect it to be returned to me without delay.

"I am unable to come in person for the money but my messenger will call at your home tomorrow at three o'clock. Have it ready for him, and signify your intention of doing so by replying to this note.

John Ely."

"Oh, dear, I've been afraid something like this would happen," Mrs. Doke murmured.

"If I were you I shouldn't be too hasty about turning over the money," Professor Crandall advised, before either of the Dana girls could voice a similar sentiment. "This man may prove to be an impostor."

"Then what shall I do about replying? If I flatly refuse to give up the property he may sue me. I couldn't bear the publicity."

While Mrs. Doke was discussing the matter with the Crandalls in an attempt to reach a decision, the Dana girls went to the front door to interview the boy who had brought the note. He did not answer their questions satisfactorily and would give them no information regarding the man whom he served.

"But where are you to meet him when you carry back Mrs. Doke's note?" Jean persisted.

"I can't tell you that," the boy replied with a shrug. "I can't tell you anything. If I do I won't be paid."

The Dana girls returned to the living room, more suspicious than ever of the writer of the note, and certain that he was an impostor. They added their argument to that of the Crandalls, urging Mrs. Doke to use the utmost caution in her dealings with the man.

"I don't know what to write to him," Mrs. Doke said uneasily.

"Why not say that you cannot turn over the money unless he is able to prove conclusively that he is John Ely?" Louise advised. "If the man has a just claim, the request will not seem unreasonable to him."

"An excellent suggestion," Mrs. Crandall said.

"If the messenger should return the note to John Ely we could follow him and see where he goes," Jean added. "I don't like all this mystery which surrounds the man. He seems to be afraid to show his face."

Mrs. Doke wrote the note as her friends dictated and then handed it to the messenger boy. Louise and Jean waited until he was some distance from the house, then cautiously shadowed him.

The lad took a street car to the outskirts of the city. Never suspecting that he was being followed, he walked swiftly toward the Elmo River. He entered the woods and turned in the direction of the cave. The Dana girls were wondering if that could be his destination, when he took a different trail and eventually paused by a cliff.

"Evidently he plans to meet John Ely here," Jean whispered, as they watched from behind the bushes.

In this expectation she was not correct. They saw the boy grope along the rocky wall until he came to a half-hidden ledge. He ran his hand beneath it and drew out a dollar bill. He thrust the money into his pocket and in its place laid the note from Mrs. Doke. Then he hurried off through the woods, whistling cheerfully.

"John Ely must be planning to come here

for the message when he feels it is safe,''
Louise commented. ''Shall we wait?''

''Of course.''

The girls found a comfortable place screened
by the bushes and sat down to wait. Half an
hour elapsed. Far down the trail they heard
voices. Instantly Louise and Jean became
alert.

''That can't be John Ely,'' Louise whispered.

Two girls came into view, walking wearily
along the path. The Danas drew deeper into
the bushes as they recognized Lettie Briggs
and her companion, Ina Mason. They hoped
that the pair would walk past them without
glancing in either direction. To their dismay,
Ina and Lettie sat down to rest near the ledge
where Mrs. Doke's note had been hidden.

''I'm thoroughly disgusted that we lost that
old map!'' Lettie commented irritably. ''I feel
sure it would have led us to a treasure. What
fun to have discovered it and then played a
joke on the Dana girls by carrying it away!''

''It doesn't do any good to think about it
now,'' Ina responded gloomily. ''We can't
even find the cave.''

''We'll find it if we have to hunt for it the
rest of our lives! We can't be far from the
place now.''

The pair arose as if to continue down the
trail. But to the dismay of the Dana girls,

Lettie's eye was drawn to the half-hidden shelf in the cliff. She uttered a triumphant cry of discovery.

"See what I've found, Ina! A note!"

"Let's read it."

"It's sealed."

"What's the difference? We found it, didn't we?"

Jean and Louise had no choice now but to emerge from their hiding place to claim the message. Lettie and Ina were startled at the girls' unexpected appearance but they stood their ground undaunted.

"Please, Lettie," Louise said politely. "We left that message for another person."

"You don't say?" Lettie smiled insultingly. "Your boy friend, perhaps?"

"No, it wasn't our boy friend!" Jean retorted. "This is a strictly business matter."

"I've never heard of business letters being hidden under rocks!"

"That's beside the point, Lettie," Louise said impatiently. "Please give us the note."

"I don't know why I should; at least, not without an explanation. While you're about it you might tell me what you hid in the cave, too!"

"This affair is none of your concern, Lettie," Louise said with growing irritation.

"Perhaps I choose to make it so!"

Jean, unable to bear such an unreasonable attitude, suddenly dived forward and snatched the note from the surprised Lettie.

"I didn't want the thing anyway!" the Briggs girl said angrily. "I intended to give it back all the time. I only thought it would be fun to get you excited."

"Let me tell you something about this note," Louise Dana replied severely. "Mrs. Crandall helped write it. If you insist upon making further trouble, you may have to answer to her!"

As she had anticipated, the mention of Mrs. Crandall's name had its effect upon Lettie.

"Oh, come on, Ina," she muttered with a pretense of indifference. "Let's go back to Starhurst. Who cares about this silly old message?"

They hastily quit the scene.

"Lettie is afraid she'll get into serious difficulties with Mrs. Crandall," Jean chuckled, as she and Louise replaced the note in the ledge. "I suspect she and Ina left the school today without permission."

Scarcely had the girls secreted the message when they again heard footsteps coming down the trail. They crouched low among the bushes and waited, wondering if Ina and Lettie were returning.

A colored man came into view, shuffling along

with uncertain gait. He halted, and looked about him in all directions. Satisfied that he was alone in the woods, he slowly circled a rock pile which had been heaped up near the cliff. While the girls marveled at this strange action, he moved on to the ledge. There he thrust in his hand and drew forth the note.

Without attempting to read the message, he put it into his coat pocket. Then he walked rapidly away through the darkening woods.

Jean and Louise emerged from their hiding place. "What do you make of it?" the latter demanded in bewilderment. "Did he find that note by accident, or can he be John Ely?"

"I never thought John Ely would be a colored man, Louise. Shall we follow him?"

"I don't believe it would do any good. It will be too dark within fifteen minutes to keep him in sight."

"I guess we should be getting back," Jean acknowledged.

"First, I'd like to examine that man's footprints. Did you notice the odd way he circled the rock pile?"

"Yes, I did, Louise. It reminded me of the masked thief. But that man was *white*."

"We don't know that he was," Louise corrected. "Naturally we made such an assumption, but you recall the time when he came to Mrs. Doke's home he wore a mask. At Starhurst it was too dark for anyone to see his face plainly.''

''But the peddler who annoyed Aunt Harriet was white——''

''We have no proof that he was the same masked thief. However, I think you may be right, Jean. This fellow easily could have blackened his face with cork.''

''Let's examine the tracks right away or it will be too dark to see them,'' Jean proposed.

They moved toward the rock pile where the circling footprints were faintly visible in the loose earth. Jean stooped down to measure several of them.

''Louise, they're exactly the same length as those other footprints! I am sure of that!''

''They do look identical.''

''Then it's fairly evident that this man who claims to be John Ely is the masked thief!''

''The evidence seems to point to that,'' Louise agreed cautiously. ''Of course, two men could easily wear the same size shoe.''

''But these footprints are in a *circle,* the same as those we found at the house and by the fountain! It's more than just mere coincidence, it seems to me.''

''I wish we had attempted to follow the man,'' Louise said regretfully. ''It's too late now.''

Alarmed at the rapidity with which night was

coming on, the girls started to retrace their way through the woods. They had gone scarcely a dozen yards when they were startled to hear a man's hoarse cry for help. The sound seemed to come from the vicinity of the river.

"What was that?" Jean demanded, halting.

"I heard a splash! Someone—probably that colored man—has fallen into the river!"

The girls turned and ran in the direction from whence had come the call. Approaching the steep bank of the Elmo, they saw a dark form floundering about in the water below. It was impossible for them to tell whether the man was swimming awkwardly or struggling desperately to remain afloat. At any rate, his wild thrashing in the water served to keep him from sinking.

"It's the colored man!" Louise exclaimed. "But if our suspicions are correct he won't be dark long. The color will wash off."

Jean caught her sister by the hand, pulling her down the steep bank toward the river.

"This is our chance to learn his true identity!" she cried. "Even if he doesn't need help, we're going to rescue him!"

CHAPTER XV

An Attempted Rescue

JEAN spoke in a louder tone than she had intended. Her words carried to the man in the water below. Turning on his back, he allowed the current to carry him swiftly downstream.

By the time the Danas reached the lower bank level he had vanished. In the gathering darkness they did not notice that he had floated into the yawning mouth of a cave, and furthermore they had no suspicion that this was another opening to the same cavern which they had explored days before. Anxiously the girls ran up and down the muddy bank, peering into the swirling water.

"He can't have gone down, Louise! We saw him swimming just a moment ago!"

"And we heard no cry—only his first yell when he slipped."

"He must have climbed out somewhere along the stream."

Once inside the cave, the man who was causing such worry chuckled to himself. He could hear the girls' conversation and enjoyed their bewilderment over his mysterious disappearance. Not until they had left the vicinity did he emerge from his hiding place.

Jean and Louise returned reluctantly to the Doke cottage, troubled by the incident, yet firmly convinced that the colored man had not drowned. Upon learning that Professor and Mrs. Crandall had gone back to Starhurst, they gave Mrs. Doke a hasty account of what they had witnessed, and then hurried on to the school.

No word was heard from the mysterious John Ely the following day. His silence was attributed to the demand that he furnish suitable credentials before claiming any part of the treasure.

Satisfied that the man would make no trouble for a time at least, Louise and Jean continued their search for Julia Bellington and the next person on the list, Jane Judson. Jean had read of a well-known Judson family which chanced to be connected with the manufacture of airplanes.

With this clue in mind, the girls attended an air meet in a nearby city. There, after considerable inquiry, they located Mr. Judson of the Judson Air Line, and were overjoyed to learn from him that his wife's name was Jane.

"My wife was always gullible about investments," Mr. Judson told the girls. "I don't doubt but that this fellow Doke cheated her out of six thousand dollars. If you want to talk to my wife, I'll fly you down to our summer home at Albion. She's staying there now."

Gratefully Jean and Louise accepted the offer. The journey by air was thrilling, and they were greatly impressed by the beautiful estate where the Judson family resided. The owner landed his plane at a private field.

"Just run on up to the house while I attend to having the plane refueled," he said carelessly. "My wife will greet you with open arms."

This last remark, Louise and Jean soon discovered, was a figure of speech. Mrs. Judson did not welcome them with open arms nor even courteously. Having no idea of why the girls were calling, the woman frowned as a maid admitted them to her private sitting room.

"I can give you only three minutes," she said coldly. "I am a very busy woman. I suppose it's a donation you want."

"We have come to bestow money, not to ask for it," Louise smiled.

"There's some trick to it, of course. There always is. I have given away far too much money as it is. I really wouldn't be interested in any proposition which you may have to offer."

Jean and Louise made several attempts to explain the purpose of their call, but Mrs. Jud-

son would not listen. She was about to dismiss
them from her presence when her husband arrived and made it clear that the girls were his
guests. Not until then did the arrogant woman
give them an opportunity to talk.

Upon hearing that she was to receive six
thousand dollars Mrs. Judson's manner under-
went an amusing change. She could not be nice
enough to the girls. The interview ended
pleasantly, with Louise and Jean satisfied that
the woman actually had been cheated by Mason
Doke.

They were just leaving when a butler chanced
to pass the open doorway. Louise recognized
him as the man who had pushed Casey Riley
downstairs. Feeling that it was her duty to
warn the Judsons, she revealed what she knew
about him.

The society woman readily admitted that the
servant had been employed only two days before. However, she did not thank Louise for
warning her. Mr. Judson's attitude was far
different.

"We'll get rid of that man at once!" he
promised the Dana girls. "I thought he was a
suspicious character when my wife engaged
him. As I entered the house a few minutes
ago I found him examining the silverware."

"But that is one of his duties," Mrs. Judson
replied in a bored tone.

"My dear," her husband returned severely, "this is one time when I must overrule you. The man will be discharged."

"Oh, very well, have it your own way."

Mr. Judson assured the girls of his gratitude, not only for the information regarding the butler, but also for guaranteeing the return of the Doke money to his wife.

"I wish I might repay the favor," he remarked.

"Perhaps you can tell us where to find some of the other people on our list," Jean said jokingly. "The name of one is Samuel Slayback."

Mr. Judson's face broke into a smile.

"Why, there is a restaurant proprietor in this town by that name! I will have my chauffeur take you there."

The girls were jubilant at their good fortune in tracing Mr. Slayback with such little effort. Soon they were riding in the luxurious Judson limousine toward the business section of Albion.

The car drew up before a brick building which housed several apartments and shops. Jean and Louise alighted, and looked through a dingy plate-glass window which bore the painted sign:

"SLAYBACK'S SPA."

"Why, the interior is empty!"

The girls tried the front door only to find it

locked. They stepped into an adjoining meat market to ask the butcher if he could give them any information about Samuel Slayback.

"Creditors closed his place up last week," the man replied. "They say Slayback skipped the town. If you want to learn the details, why not have a talk with his mother? She lives in one of the apartments upstairs."

Louise and Jean did not overlook this lead. Presently they were admitted to a comfortable though modest three-room suite directly over the restaurant. They observed at once that the white-haired old lady who bade them enter had been weeping. She could not restrain her sobs when Jean asked her if they might have her son's new address.

"I only wish I knew where to find him. Samuel felt disgraced over his business failure. He tried very hard to make the business a success but everyone was against him. When creditors closed him out he went all to pieces. He talked of sailing for Africa on a tramp steamer. I am afraid he may have carried out his threat."

This information was disheartening to Louise and Jean. Moreover, they failed to cheer the mother by their news that they had come to pay Samuel Slayback.

"What a pity that the money should come too late," she said sadly. "Last week three thousand dollars would have saved his business.''

The girls lingered a few minutes longer, trying to bring comfort to the discouraged woman.

"There is a possibility we may locate your son yet," Louise declared as they bade her goodbye. "Our uncle is captain of an ocean liner, and through him we may be able to learn if Mr. Slayback secured passage aboard a tramp steamer.''

The Dana girls really had slight hope that Uncle Ned would be able to accomplish such a feat, but that night upon their return to Starhurst they sent him a wire. Several days elapsed, and then one afternoon they received a surprising response.

"Samuel Slayback located. He returns home tomorrow.''

Louise and Jean immediately telephoned Mrs. Slayback the good news and the following day received permission to visit the woman. They found her enjoying a happy reunion with her son. The young man looked haggard and worn from the strain of the past few weeks, but otherwise seemed to be in excellent spirits.

His mother had told him the purpose of the Dana girls' call. Louise and Jean asked several questions and became convinced that his claim to the Doke money was a sound one.

"How soon may I have the three thousand

dollars?" Mr. Slayback inquired eagerly. "It's just possible that if I could get it within a few days I might be able to save my business."

"I think we can close the transaction very quickly," Louise promised. "We will be able to send you the money whenever Mrs. Doke approves the settlement."

The doorbell sounded just as the girls were turning to leave. Mrs. Slayback answered the summons.

"Oh, dear, it's that horrid man Cohan," she reported in an undertone to her son.

"My chief creditor," Mr. Slayback explained to Louise and Jean. "A man from Penfield. I'll tell him I can soon pay the amount I owe."

The girls were startled to hear the familiar name and even more astonished when Mr. Cohan walked briskly into the apartment. He was indeed the same man who had caused Joe Doke to lose his position at the telegraph office. Cohan scarcely bestowed a glance upon Louise and Jean, so determined was he to make short work of the business at hand.

"I'm glad to find you at home, Slayback," he said unpleasantly. "I've brought all the papers. You have no choice but to sign everything over to me."

"It happens that I can guarantee to settle what I owe."

"Ridiculous!" Mr. Cohan snapped. "Your restaurant is closed. You haven't a dime in the bank. You are very fortunate that I am willing to take the restaurant and fixtures off your hands in settlement for the note."

"I'll have three thousand dollars within a few days."

"You expect me to believe such a story?"

"It is the truth," Jean confirmed. "My sister and I are agents for a woman who is paying Mr. Slayback exactly that sum."

Mr. Cohan turned to stare at the two girls, for the first time recognizing them. His bird-like eyes gleamed with anger and hatred. In a tone tense with suppressed emotion he warned harshly:

"So! You interfere again! If you're wise you'll keep out of this!"

He turned abruptly and rushed out of the apartment, banging the door.

CHAPTER XVI

A Grateful Family

Undaunted by the warning, Louise and Jean went ahead with their plan to pay three thousand dollars over to Mr. Slayback. Cohan's threat only served to strengthen their determination to save the restaurant from the wily creditor.

General inquiry revealed that Samuel Slayback was a hard working, honest young man, whereas Mr. Cohan had few scruples in his business dealings. Through the druggist where Joe Doke worked, the Dana girls learned that the man, though still holding a position with the telegraph company, was ambitious to become the owner of a restaurant chain. It had long been Cohan's policy to force restaurant proprietors out of business by lending them money and then providing ruinous competition.

Cohan especially coveted the Slayback Spa, which was in an unusually desirable location. It was not surprising in the least that he bitterly resented the timely interference of the Dana girls. When they delivered the three thousand dollars to Samuel Slayback his anger knew no bounds. However, there was nothing he could do but agree to accept payment for the notes due him, and relinquish all claim to the restaurant.

Following the successful conclusion of this transaction, Louise and Jean devoted themselves to school examinations. Despite the fact that they had absented themselves from many classes, their work had not seriously suffered; their corrected papers came back with satisfactory grades.

Louise and Jean began to consider ways and means of locating the next person whose name appeared upon the Doke list. According to the memorandum in their possession, Mrs. Mary Tito was to receive five thousand dollars. The girls had no idea where to find her.

They were discussing the situation one afternoon while they rested under the shade of an elm tree on the school lawn. Presently a well-dressed man with a suitcase paused beside them.

"I wonder if you could tell me where to find Miss Briggs?" he inquired.

"Lettie Briggs?" Jean asked.

"Yes, I am her father. I suppose she told you I was coming to visit her."

Louise and Jean were chagrined to discover themselves staring at the man. They had never seen Mr. Briggs before, and were surprised to see that he was so very nice looking. Now that they came to think of it, they did recall that Lettie had told everyone in school that her father expected to pay her a visit.

"Lettie went to the airport today," Jean replied. "I remember hearing her say she was to meet someone there."

"It was my fault that I missed her. I wired that I was coming by plane. Then I lost my courage and traveled by train instead. You see, I was in a recent airplane accident, and since then I've been nervous."

Louise and Jean nodded sympathetically. They did not reveal that their uncle was captain of the *Balaska*.

"We read about the accident," Louise commented. "You were acquainted with the pilot, I believe."

"Only in a business way. I felt sorry for the poor fellow, but it really was not my fault that he met with the mishap, even though I knew he would fly over the ship."

"Didn't he dive low to signal to you?" Jean questioned in a casual voice.

"Yes, it was in regard to a business matter. The fellow's death deeply shocked me. It disrupted all our plans."

"Perhaps it was fortunate that they could never be carried out," Louise commented.

"What do you mean?"

"Surely you know that Mason Doke was a notorious forger?"

"Certainly not! He came to me highly recommended. I intended to enter a bond deal with him. Why, this is astounding!"

The Dana girls were revealing additional facts, when they were disconcerted by having Lettie appear. She had waited in vain for her father at the airport, and was now returning to Starhurst in a disagreeable mood. Coming up quietly behind the group, she overheard several remarks which concerned Mason Doke.

"Don't you believe a word of it, Dad," she interrupted. "The Dana girls always tell fantastic tales. They have a reputation for that sort of thing."

"The Dana girls?" Mr. Briggs echoed in astonishment. "Nieces of Captain Ned Dana?"

"Of course. I've already written to you about them."

The friendly expression completely faded from Mr. Briggs's face. Louise and Jean knew that his opinion of them had been formed from his daughter's highly-colored reports.

"Oh, I see!" he said coldly. "Let us go, Lettie."

The matter did not end there, however. Mr. Briggs went directly to Professor and Mrs. Crandall, reporting what he considered to be the outrageous conduct of the Dana girls.

Louise and Jean were called to the office to explain their side of the situation. They repeated the conversation which had taken place and felt justly triumphant when Mrs. Crandall assured Lettie's father that everything said about Mason Doke was the absolute truth. Mr. Briggs apologized to the girls, an act which deeply humiliated Lettie.

During the following week Louise and Jean spent many hours at the Doke cottage. They harbored a hope that the mysterious John Ely might call to press his claims, for since the first message from him had arrived two others had come. The notes gave positive proof that the man had not drowned in the Elmo River. Other than that, the girls gleaned nothing of value from them. Ely continued to press his claim to the money, yet offered no evidence to substantiate his demands.

In the meantime, Louise and Jean ran down many fruitless clues regarding the whereabouts of Mrs. Mary Tito. One evening while attending a concert in Penfield they were startled to observe that the name *Alice Tito* appeared on the program. They waited expectantly for her to appear.

Miss Tito was a beautiful young woman with a brilliant smile which captivated the audience. She entertained her listeners with difficult piano selections, winning many rounds of applause.

Louise and Jean listened enthralled to the music, but the moment Miss Tito left the stage they, too, slipped away. A little later they succeeded in gaining admittance to the pianist's dressing room, where they were graciously received. Miss Tito did not resent their inquiry into her private affairs.

"Why yes, I can tell you how to find Mary Tito," she responded. "She is my mother."

Before the Dana girls left an hour later they had gleaned the facts of Miss Tito's life. It was a story of hardship and struggle. At ten years of age the girl had been proclaimed a prodigy. She had been launched upon a promising musical career, but the death of her father and resulting financial reverses had made it increasingly difficult for her to go on with her studies.

Mrs. Mary Tito had worked very hard to provide money for the necessary musical education. A five-thousand-dollar fund which was to be used for study in Europe had been misappropriated by a certain Mason Doke, who had convinced Mrs. Tito that he could make quick profits by investing the money and thus adding materially to the capital.

"Now I am trying to build up the fund again," Miss Tito sighed. "I earn a few dollars each night with these professional engagements. It is a long, hard road, and I should have failed dismally had it not been for Sigmond Darlias, the famous pianist. He has been giving me free lessons.''

The girls were about to tell Miss Tito of the good fortune awaiting her, but were prevented from doing so by the appearance of a distinguished looking gentleman in the open doorway of the dressing room.

''Ah, Miss Tito,'' he smiled in greeting. ''Do I interrupt?''

''Not at all, Mr. Darlias. Please come in.''

Miss Tito presented the musician to the girls.

''You did splendidly tonight!'' the teacher praised his pupil. ''Splendidly!''

Miss Tito flushed with pleasure. ''Thank you. I owe my technique entirely to your training, Mr. Darlias.''

A frown puckered the teacher's brow. ''Ah, that is what brought me here. I am sorry to have to tell you, but I can no longer give you lessons.''

Miss Tito appeared stunned, then recovered her composure.

''I understand,'' she said at length. ''You have given so generously of your time. I cannot expect you to keep on without remuneration.''

''Oh, that is not my reason,'' replied Mr. Darlias. ''It has been a genuine pleasure to aid you, Miss Tito. Never have I had a student so talented. I should like to continue our work together, but unfortunately I must consider my own future. I have been asked to go on tour, and will not return to this place for two years.''

''I am glad to hear this,'' smiled Miss Tito. ''I am sorry, though, not to be able to continue my lessons.''

Louise stepped forward, her eyes shining.

''You need not give up your lessons, Miss Tito,'' she announced. ''My sister and I came here to tell you that the five thousand dollars stolen by Mason Doke will be returned to your mother!''

Miss Tito's sadness vanished as if by magic. She was triumphant now. She might go to New York, or even abroad, to study.

''Do you realize what this means, Sigmond Darlias?'' she demanded of her astonished teacher.

''I do indeed,'' he replied, bowing low. ''You shall one day be a supreme artist!''

CHAPTER XVII

THE PERFUME THIEF

THE next day the Dana girls escorted the happy Miss Tito to the home of Mrs. Doke, there to make arrangements for receiving the money due her mother. After various matters had been settled, Louise timidly requested the talented young pianist to favor the group with a few selections.

Miss Tito graciously responded, pretending not to notice that the old piano was out of tune and that some of the keys stuck. As it would be impossible to play any difficult numbers, she tried simple melodies, launching finally into well-known songs. In the midst of this, Joe quietly took from an old case a flute. He began to play with the woman, gathering confidence as they went on.

Miss Tito glanced with startled eyes toward the boy. As the last note died slowly away she whirled about to face the little group.

"Why, this boy has talent. Who is his teacher?"

"He has none," Mrs. Doke admitted. "Joe has always liked to play, but I never could afford to provide him with any instruction. When he was a little fellow his father showed him how to blow and make the sounds.''

"It is a pity not to develop such talent! I have a friend, an excellent teacher, who might help him.''

Tears gleamed in Mrs. Doke's eyes as she thanked Miss Tito. Joe was fairly overwhelmed by the musician's kindness. While she remained at the cottage his worshipful gaze seldom left her face.

The following week the boy went about in a semi-dazed state, still thrilled by his good fortune. He became slightly less attentive in his duties at the drug store, although he continued to serve the customers efficiently.

But trouble lay ahead for Joe. He had no suspicion that anything was amiss when Lettie Briggs entered and sat down at one of the tables. The girl had learned that the lad was the son of Mason Doke, and it was her intention to make life miserable for Joe.

Lettie ordered a chocolate soda. When it was brought to her she flew into a temper, declaring loudly that she had requested a sundae. Joe hastily made the exchange, but after the girl had gone he was reprimanded by the store owner for his "mistake.''

Later in the day Ina Mason dropped into the pharmacy. The little act was repeated with slight variations, and again Joe was blamed for a supposed blunder.

"I should think you would be afraid to keep that boy in the store," Ina commented to the druggist as she paid her bill. "The son of a forger!"

The proprietor was disturbed by the reference to Joe's father. He might have overlooked it, had it not been for a loss which he had discovered the night before in checking over his perfume stock. Two bottles of valuable cologne were missing.

Joe could not explain what had become of them. He vaguely remembered that a colored man had looked at some expensive perfume the previous day, but had gone away without making a purchase.

"I believe you took the perfume yourself!" the druggist accused Joe severely. "I should have known better than to hire the son of a forger!"

Joe frantically protested his innocence. The druggist, irritated by the mistakes in soda counter orders which had been made that day, refused to listen, and he coldly discharged the boy.

Sick with discouragement, Joe arrived home to find the Dana girls in conversation with his mother. They listened sympathetically while he poured forth his tale of woe.

"Lettie and Ina are back of it all!" Jean commented indignantly. "Maybe they took the perfume, too."

"Ina and Lettie are downright mean, but I doubt they would actually steal," Louise added reflectively.

To console Joe, who felt that he would never secure another position until he had been cleared of the theft charge, the girls promised to do everything in their power to right the wrong. Actually, they had slight hope of ever tracing the person who had stolen the perfume.

At Starhurst the next day Louise and Jean made inquiry regarding the tastes which Lettie and Ina displayed in perfume. They were surprised to find that the two girls favored very inexpensive varieties.

"That excuses them," Jean said. "Joe is probably right in thinking they didn't steal the store perfume."

"No one around the dormitory uses cologne noticeably except Amanda," Louise remarked with a smile. "She loves it, though."

Jean stared at her sister.

"Amanda, the cook? What makes you think she uses it?"

"She was passing through the hall on her way to the kitchen a few minutes ago. One could detect the scent a block away!"

"Then probably it was cheap perfume."

"It wasn't cheap, Jean, but she had used it in generous quantities."

Jean arose abruptly, saying with a smile, "Your information intrigues me. Behold, I go to investigate!"

Louise did not consider it worth her while to accompany her sister to the kitchen. She was engrossed in her algebra when Jean came hurrying back, greatly excited.

"Louise, I've just learned something important from Amanda! You were right about that perfume. It is an expensive variety."

"I hope you don't intend to pin the theft upon poor Amanda, Jean."

"Of course not. But do you know where she got it?"

"I'm not a mind reader, so I can't say."

"The perfume was a gift from her colored gentleman friend, Algernon Prentice!" Jean announced impressively. "Amanda told me too that he often does errands for the drug store—the one where Joe worked."

By this time Louise was deeply impressed. She tossed aside her book and began to ask eager questions.

"Amanda didn't suspect why I was so interested," Jean went on. "She gave me Algernon's address. I'm going there now to see what I can find out."

"And I'm going with you!"

Algernon Prentice's cottage, a tumble-down affair with sagging roof and broken windows, stood on the outskirts of the town. Algernon himself sat tilted back in a chair on the porch, contentedly smoking a corncob pipe.

The Dana girls were too clever to make a direct accusation or even to mention the perfume. They began their conversation in an indirect fashion, encouraging the negro to make various revelations. Soon he was talking freely of his great affection for Amanda and of his desire to shower luxuries upon her.

"I nevah has enough money to gib her de things her heart craves," he said regretfully. "Mandy's de cravenest gal you evah did see, 'specially fo' perfume. She jest drenches herself in it. Dat gal smells like a flower store half de time. I is a hard wo'kin' man but de lady I wo'ks for sometimes thinks I don't need any money de way she holds out on mah pay. But I suah do need it to keep Mandy goin'. Sometimes mah fingers feel sticky—like I might take things that belongs to other folks."

"Such as perfume?" Louise supplied carelessly.

"Yes ma'am! No, I takes dat back! Not dat stuff!" Algernon checked himself quickly, realizing he had made a damaging admission.

"It's no use to deny it, Algernon," Jean said severely. "We have proof that you stole ex-

pensive perfume from the Henderson drug
store in Penfield. Now, unless you do exactly
as we ask, you'll be turned over to the police.''

Poor Algernon did not question the quality
of the ''proof'' which stood against him. At
first he falteringly denied that he had taken the
perfume, but soon broke down and made a complete confession.

''I took it, Miss,'' he admitted. ''I done it
for Amanda. Dat gal was goin' to ditch me if
I didn't bring her somethin' sweet-smellin'. I
didn't mean no harm.''

''You must go to the druggist and tell him
everything,'' Louise insisted. ''If you do that,
we'll try to protect you and save you from the
police.''

''I is willin' to do anything you says,'' Algernon agreed submissively, ''only don't tell de
old woman I wo'k for. She'll have a spasm,
suah. Miss McKinley's always carryin' on,
anyway.''

''McKinley?'' Jean inquired alertly. ''Is
that the name of your employer?''

''Dat's right. Miss Barbara McKinley. She
lives all alone and don't like it when folks come
to see her.''

The Dana girls did not alarm Algernon by
telling him that they intended to call upon the
woman without delay. The colored man's information had excited them, and they were

hopeful that Barbara McKinley might prove to be the person whom they were seeking in regard to the Doke money.

Upon leaving the cottage they walked swiftly down the winding road, now and then pausing at a house to inquire where Miss McKinley lived. They were directed to an unsightly habitation, set far back from the highway in a grove of pine trees. The old building had not been painted in years; many of the shutters were missing; bricks had fallen from the chimney.

Jean knocked firmly on the front door. After waiting for several minutes the girls walked around to the rear and rapped again.

"Miss McKinley doesn't seem to be at home," Louise remarked in disappointment.

"Perhaps she won't come to the door. Algernon said she didn't like visitors."

"We may as well go back to Starhurst."

"Wait a minute, Louise. The side door is slightly ajar."

"Then she must be around here somewhere."

"Perhaps Miss McKinley is deaf and didn't hear our knock. Let's look in and see if anyone is at home."

"I don't know if we should——"

"Oh, why not, Louise? We'll do no harm."

Without giving her sister an opportunity to protest, Jean pushed open the sagging door and daringly stepped into the house.

CHAPTER XVIII

A House of Mystery

LOUISE, who could not bear to be left behind, came close at Jean's heels. They huddled together just inside the door, peering about in the dim interior of the ancient house. Overhead they heard a slight noise.

"What was that?" Jean whispered nervously.

"It sounded like someone walking over a creaking board."

"Perhaps it was Miss McKinley. I'll call to her."

Jean shouted the name. It echoed weirdly, but there was no response. Still, they were certain they could hear someone moving about on tiptoe.

"She's hiding from us," Louise whispered.

This conviction grew upon the girls as they moved along the dark, narrow hall. They saw no one, yet they sensed that they were being watched.

Throughout the entire lower floor the blinds were closed. The rooms were dark. Until their eyes grew accustomed to the dim light,

Louise and Jean tripped and stumbled as they came in contact with pieces of furniture.

Nothing seemed to be in its logical place. A sofa stood at a rakish angle in the center of the room, chairs were scattered about in hit-or-miss fashion, and a small tea table had been overturned. In one spot the floor boards had rotted away, revealing damp earth beneath. The entire house had a musty, unpleasant odor.

After calling Miss McKinley's name several times, the Dana girls cautiously climbed the stairway to the second floor. They could find no one there, though it seemed to them that somebody was moving about downstairs.

"Let's get away from here and return another time," Louise suggested. "There's a weirdness about this house I don't like."

Jean was quite willing to leave. They breathed easier as they emerged into the fresh air. Suddenly Louise gripped her sister's hand and pointed to the ground.

"A circle of footprints, Jean!" she said excitedly.

Investigation disclosed that the trail went completely around the house. The prints, when measured, appeared to be identical with those which the girls had examined at other locations.

"Who could have made them?" Jean asked in stark bewilderment. "Surely not Miss McKinley."

"I don't believe the footprints were here when we first came. We would have noticed them."

"No, someone has been prowling about since our arrival. While we were in the house I sensed that we were being watched—perhaps by that masked thief."

"So did I, Jean, and I have that very same feeling now."

Nervously the girls glanced about them, but as far as they could tell they were alone. Yet it would be easy for a person to hide in the pine grove.

"We've done enough exploring for one day," Louise announced in a strained tone. "Let's get back to Starhurst."

It was nearly a week before the girls even talked of returning to the old house. Neither of them cared to admit it to the other, but for some reason they both dreaded the meeting with the eccentric Miss McKinley. They kept postponing the interview, making the excuse that their school work kept them too busy.

However, they did find time to see that Algernon Prentice made a complete confession of his theft. They interceded in his behalf, and were gratified when the druggist not only agreed to make no report of the matter to the police, but promised to reinstate Joe Doke in his former position.

In the midst of school examinations a letter arrived from Captain Dana, telling the girls that Casey Riley was enjoying his ocean voyage and seemed vastly improved in health. The only discouraging item was an enclosure from him mentioning his regret at being unable to find a trace of Julia Bellington. He had not given up the search, however. Upon his return to the United States he had every intention of assisting the Danas in locating the woman.

"If we find Miss Bellington and succeed in contacting Barbara McKinley, our work will have been finished," Jean remarked. "I'll be almost glad to see the end of that list."

"There's one complication which I think we're overlooking," Louise said soberly, "and that's John Ely."

From the first both girls had been concerned over the man's insistent claim to the Doke money. Of late his notes had taken on a more threatening tone. Mrs. Doke repeatedly wrote replies requesting the man to call, but he never did. At times she was convinced that he was a fraud; then again she would worry for fear his claims might be just.

"By giving away all this money we may be involving ourselves in a dreadful legal tangle," Louise commented thoughtfully to her sister. "Did it ever occur to you that Mason Doke may have lied?"

"We know that he did that many times, Louise."

"I mean, he may have told a falsehood about the money found in the Doke home. While the possibility seems remote, it's plausible at least that Doke just stumbled into that chest bearing John Ely's name. Perhaps it was buried in the cellar when the Doke family moved into the house. Mason simply appropriated it, and at the time of his death decided to make use of the money to square himself with those seven victims."

"If your theory is correct, Louise, everything will be in a hopeless muddle!"

"Oh, I'm not saying I have faith in such a theory. I really believe Ely is an impostor—but I can't help worrying just the same."

Jean sat lost in deep thought for a time. Suddenly she sprang to her feet, elated by an idea. "Louise, I know how we can solve the mystery!" she cried.

"How? By asking a fortune teller?"

"By consulting the tax office!" Jean cried triumphantly. "We can easily find out if a man named John Ely ever owned the Doke house!"

"But the man may have only rented it. Still, it is a good lead—one we've overlooked."

The girls lost no time in visiting the local tax office. They were forced to make several trips before they finally gleaned the information they sought; yet in the end they were glad that they had made the necessary effort, for their findings were valuable even though somewhat alarming.

According to the records of the tax office, John Ely had owned the Doke property for eight years, residing at the cottage until the time of his death. Following his demise, the house had been sold completely furnished to a real estate company. It was from this concern that the Dokes had rented the property.

"This sheds light upon the situation," Louise remarked as she and Jean discussed their new information, "but the mystery is as deep as ever."

Jean nodded soberly.

"It's all a dreadful tangle. If John Ely did die, then it's clear this man who annoys Mrs. Doke is an impostor. On the other hand, if a man by the name of Ely formerly owned the house, it's quite probable that he left that chest of money buried in the cellar."

"And there's no way of finding out how many relatives Mr. Ely may have," Louise added gloomily. "Any one of them may show up to establish a just claim to the chest."

"Nearly all the money has been given away, too. What are we to do?"

"What can we do except carry on according to Mrs. Doke's instructions?" Louise asked. "At least we should contact Miss McKinley and then allow Mrs. Doke to decide whether or not to give her the money."

"I guess that's the only way. We really should call on Miss McKinley. We've postponed our trip far too long."

That very day the girls set out for the old house on the outskirts of Penfield. They noticed that several upstairs windows were open, even though all the blinds on the first floor were closed. They were therefore encouraged to believe that the owner was at home. However, their knock went unanswered.

"This is provoking!" Jean exclaimed irritably. "Here we've made another long trip for nothing. I know that woman is inside!"

She tried the door only to find it locked.

"I heard someone moving about inside," Louise whispered, "and I thought I saw a face at the window!"

"I've had quite enough of this hide-and-seek game! Even if I'm arrested for house-breaking, I'm going in there and find that woman!" said Jean determinedly.

Before Louise could dissuade her sister from such a daring undertaking, Jean had discovered that one blind was not fastened and the window was unlocked. She quickly opened it and climbed in. After some hesitation Louise reluctantly followed.

"There's no one here," Jean whispered as they huddled together, listening.

The girls tiptoed down the hall and peered into the dark living room. Suddenly the ancient house resounded with a terrifying scream. Their hearts in their throats, the Danas recoiled against a wall.

"Ghosts! Spirits!" a voice screamed. "Go away! Leave me alone!"

From the semi-darkness the figure of a bent old woman emerged. Her face was a chalky white, and straggling gray hair streamed down over her bushy eyebrows. She carried a stout cane which she swished wildly about, striking at the furniture and curtains.

"She surely must be Miss McKinley," Jean whispered nervously. "I don't believe the woman is in her right mind."

"Don't be afraid, Miss McKinley," Louise said soothingly. "We're not ghosts."

The woman continued to advance menacingly toward them.

"I can see your evil faces shining in the dark! You can't trick me! Ghosts are always in white."

"We're wearing white clothes," Jean murmured apprehensively. "Please—Miss Mc-Kinley——"

Her words ended in a scream of pain. The old woman had moved forward with the agility of a cunning animal. She caught Jean's wrist in her gnarled hand and gave it a cruel twist.

"This is the way I deal with evil spirits!" she cackled. "I scratch and bite and make them sorry they ever came to haunt a poor old woman!"

CHAPTER XIX

Ghosts?

Jean tried to jerk herself free from the old woman, but Miss McKinley's grip held like a steel vise. Louise darted to her sister's aid, and for a few minutes the three struggled wildly. The demented woman tore at their clothing, biting and scratching as she did so.

During the mêlee furniture was overturned and a heavy picture crashed to the floor, sending up a cloud of dust. Miss McKinley began to cough and choke. Her grip on Jean's arm relaxed slightly, allowing the girl to break away.

"Ghosts! Ghosts! Ghosts!" Miss McKinley screamed, whirling about to thrash at the fallen picture with her cane.

She smashed the glass into a hundred pieces; then, apparently satisfied with this bit of destruction, she began to laugh hysterically. For the moment she seemed to forget the Dana girls. They huddled in a shadowed nook, watching her.

Miss McKinley wandered aimlessly about the room. Presently she sank into a chair, and with an abrupt change of mood she buried her withered face in her hands and began to sob.

"What have I done? What have I done?" they heard her whisper. "Why am I like this? Why must I suffer from this dreadful thing?"

After a time Miss McKinley arose wearily, and without glancing toward Louise or Jean she climbed the stairway to the second floor. They heard her enter a bedroom and lock the door.

"Now what are we to do?" Jean asked her sister.

"I'm sure I don't know," Louise returned helplessly. "We can't talk to the poor woman in her present condition."

"I think she should be in an institution."

"At least she requires the care of a trained nurse, Jean. Perhaps she'll be able to have one if we turn over the Doke money to her."

"I'll give that task to you, Louise. After our little battle I don't care for it myself. My suit is ruined. The sleeve is completely torn away."

"My skirt is ripped. But we're fortunate not to have been harmed."

With Miss McKinley safely confined to her bedroom, the time was ripe for the girls to make their escape; yet they were reluctant to leave the poor old woman alone in the house, fearing that she might attempt to harm herself.

Jean opened the blinds, which admitted the sunlight to the lower floor. Both girls were dismayed to note the dirty condition of the room.

"How can anyone live in such a place, Louise? It isn't healthful."

"Let's clean up the place a bit before we leave."

They found broom, dustpan and rags in the kitchen. Once started, there seemed to be no end to the work. The girls had straightened up the living room and were turning their attention to the kitchen when Miss McKinley's excited voice broke upon them again.

"Robbers! Thieves!" she screamed from her bedroom. "Go away! Go away!"

"Oh dear, she's at it again," Jean said despairingly.

"Perhaps if we were to give her some food, it might quiet her, and then she could go to sleep," Louise suggested.

The two searched the larder and found eggs, tea, and a few staples. Louise made an omelet while her sister brewed a hot drink. Together they carried the repast upstairs and knocked on the bedroom door.

"We've brought you something nice to eat, Miss McKinley," Louise said coaxingly. "A delicious omelet——"

"Poison! Poison!" the demented woman

shrieked. "If you try to bring it in here I'll throw it in your face."

"She would, too," Jean commented grimly.

They carried the food downstairs, and hastily finished cleaning up the kitchen. Then they prepared to leave.

"There's nothing we can do for her in her present condition," Jean said sadly. "Perhaps she'll quiet down in a few days."

Before leaving the house the girls went again to Miss McKinley's door.

"We'll return later," Louise attempted to explain. "In the meantime try to think of us as friends, for I promise you we'll bring good news when we come again."

Only a deep silence greeted these words. The girls were unable to tell whether or not the woman had heard them. As they closed the outside door behind them, Miss McKinley ran to her bedroom window and watched them until they were out of sight down the road.

"So they're coming again!" she muttered. "Barbara McKinley will be waiting!"

Donning cloak and bonnet, she cautiously unlocked her bedroom door and descended to the kitchen. She took a large market basket from the shelf, and hooking it over her arm she left the house.

The long walk to Penfield proved tiring to Miss McKinley, but her grim purpose gave her strength with which to endure the heat of the sun. She halted at the first grocery store, and after haggling with the clerk, bought ten cents worth of onions and a loaf of bread.

"A nice cake?" the clerk suggested.

Miss McKinley scrutinized the cellophane-wrapped packages and shook her head.

"The cake I buy must be a very special one," she chuckled. "One with deep frosting."

Her next call was at a bakery. There she examined a window of fine pastries, and finally, after nearly ten minutes of silent debate, she wavered in her purchase between a large chocolate cake and one with pink frosting.

"Both are fine cakes, ma'am," the clerk said wearily.

"But what kind would a young girl like best?"

"Oh, chocolate," the clerk responded carelessly.

"Then I'll take that one. Mind you, don't crush the frosting when you box it!"

With the cake reposing in the bottom of her basket, Miss McKinley next entered the drug store where Joe Doke was employed. The boy was off duty but another clerk stepped forward to wait upon her.

"I want to buy a bit of poison, young man," she said.

"Poison?" the clerk inquired cautiously. "I'm afraid we're not allowed—"

"Rat poison," Miss McKinley cut in quickly. "My house is overrun with them. A body can't stir a step but they're under foot."

"Oh, that's quite different. I thought you wanted—yes, certainly I can give you some rat poison."

He hurried to a back room. During his absence Lettie Briggs entered the store. She glanced about her irritably, and spoke petulantly when the boy returned.

"How about a little service?" she asked.

"I'll be with you in just a minute, Miss," the clerk replied.

He gave Miss McKinley her package, requesting fifty cents in payment. Immediately the old woman began to argue over the price. The clerk succeeded in being polite, but Lettie lost all patience with the customer.

"Oh, hurry up and decide if you want it or not!" she exclaimed. "There are others in this store to be served."

"You are an impertinent little snip!" Miss McKinley retorted.

She laid a fifty-cent piece on the counter. Then, picking up the package of poison, she moved toward the door.

"I'll open it for you," the clerk offered, noticing that the woman's hands were filled with packages.

Before he could reach the door Lettie, who chanced to be standing beside it, viciously pushed it ajar.

"Don't lose your rat poison!" she said jeeringly as Miss McKinley left the store.

Quick as a flash, the woman slammed the door shut on Lettie's hand. The girl jumped about, crying aloud in pain. Miss McKinley laughed derisively.

"Why, you hateful old hag! You did it on purpose!" snarled the Briggs girl.

She sprang after Miss McKinley, and in a gesture of retaliation upset the old woman's market basket. The sack of onions broke open as it struck the sidewalk, permitting the vegetables to roll about in every direction.

It was at this moment that Jean Dana arrived upon the scene. She was vastly amused to hear Lettie and poor Miss McKinley hurling bitter taunts at each other. Pedestrians began to gather. In the midst of the excitement a policeman came running up to learn what was wrong.

"Nothing at all," Lettie insisted, flushing with embarrassment. "This old woman upset her basket and she claims I did it."

"You did, too!" Miss McKinley screamed furiously. "Officer, I want you to take this mean girl to the lock-up. And there's another one that ought to go there, too.''

Her roving eye had observed Jean standing on the edge of the crowd. She pointed an accusing finger at the Dana girl.

''There she is, Officer! That girl with the yellow hair. Arrest her, too!''

CHAPTER XX

An Accusation

Miss McKinley's unexpected accusation left Jean aghast. The situation had lost its humorous aspect. She earnestly protested her innocence, but the officer seemed inclined to believe the old lady.

"These girls broke into my house this afternoon," Miss McKinley declared. "They tried to beat me and break up my furniture."

"I don't even know where this old woman lives," Lettie cut in angrily. "She must be out of her mind."

How true this was only Jean fully realized. She knew that it would be a waste of effort to attempt to make Miss McKinley tell a rational story. Obviously the woman had mistaken Lettie for Louise.

With the crowd rapidly swelling in size, the situation was growing increasingly embarrassing for both Lettie and Jean. The former tried to slip away but the officer promptly caught her by the arm, pulling her back.

"Not so fast, young lady. Maybe there's more to this than I thought!"

Both the girls became a trifle panic-stricken, fearing that the demented woman would somehow manage to send them to jail. They tried to explain how matters stood, but their stories did not carry any weight.

"Take them to the lock-up!" Miss McKinley urged spitefully. "That's where young criminals belong."

The officer was in a quandary. Jean and Lettie never had the satisfaction of knowing whether or not he would have acceded to the woman's ridiculous request, for at that critical moment a shrill cry rang out from far down the street.

"Help! Help!"

The policeman dropped Jean's arm and released Lettie. Drawing his billy club, he ran in the direction of the call. The curious crowd followed close at his heels.

"Quick, Lettie!" Jean urged. "This is our chance!"

Together the girls raced down a side street. They changed their course at the next corner and hurried toward the Starhurst campus. As they came to a street intersection they were startled to observe another girl running toward them. Her long stride soon brought her up to Lettie and Jean.

"We should all make the track team very easily!" she called out gaily. "Full speed ahead, my hearties, or that policeman will catch us yet!"

"Louise!" Jean gasped. "Why are you running?"

"For the same reason you are. So I won't be caught!"

Jean had reason to be astonished. Only a few minutes ago she had left her sister at the public library, instructing her to wait there until she should return from an errand at the drug store. Louise, however, had grown tired of standing and had walked slowly toward the pharmacy, arriving in time to discover that Jean and Lettie were involved with Miss Mc-Kinley and a policeman. Quickly retreating around a corner, Louise had called loudly for aid, hastening away when the officer answered the summons.

"Were you the person who screamed for help?" Jean asked with a chuckle.

"Guilty! But I can't run another step even if we are caught."

Louise slackened her pace and glanced back. The street was deserted.

"I think we're safe now," she decided. "That policeman is too fat to run very far."

While the girls halted to catch their breaths, she laughingly told them of her prank. For once in her life Lettie felt grateful and was far more cordial than usual to the Dana girls. The entire incident greatly excited her, appealing strongly to her sense of the dramatic. She could talk of nothing else enroute to Starhurst. Oddly enough, however, it did not occur to her to ask Jean and Louise if they were acquainted with the queer old woman.

Upon returning to the school Lettie regaled her classmates with a vivid account of Miss McKinley and her rat poison. Each time she told the tale it grew in size until Louise and Jean had no part at all in the escape from the policeman, she alone having been involved in the incident. At first the students were impressed, but finally they grew a bit bored.

Nearly everyone was amused when the story developed an unexpected anti-climax. Professor and Mrs. Crandall received a visit from the very officer who had attempted to arrest Lettie and Jean. Surmising that the girls were students at Starhurst, he requested permission to view the entire group at their general assembly. His eye passed swiftly over Jean, and finally came to rest on the trembling Lettie.

"She was the one who upset the old lady's basket," the officer indicated.

Lettie was summoned to Mrs. Crandall's office, where she was severely reprimanded for her unbecoming conduct in public. When she returned half an hour later her face was flushed and sullen.

"Any new angles to the rat story?" a classmate whispered tauntingly.

Lettie froze her with a glance. "Oh, keep still, will you?" she cried.

The following day Louise and Jean went as usual to see Mrs. Doke, whom they found in the kitchen baking apple pies.

"How good they smell!" Louise exclaimed, peering for an instant into the oven.

"You shall have one when they are ready," Mrs. Doke said. "I really baked too many."

"I don't see how we could eat a whole pie," Jean remarked. "And there's a new rule that no food may be brought into Starhurst by students."

"If you really have an extra one I know what we might do with it!" Louise cried, inspired by a sudden thought. "Why not take it to Miss McKinley?"

"She would shriek 'poison! poison!'" Jean responded without enthusiasm.

"Perhaps by this time she has quieted down a bit. The pie might help her disposition."

"I don't believe six pies would change her," Jean replied pessimistically. "It's just a waste of delicious apples."

"It might be a good idea to try Louise's suggestion," Mrs. Doke remarked, deftly transferring the pastry from the oven to the pantry shelf. "I'll be very glad to contribute the pie."

"How soon will it be cool enough to carry?"
Louise asked.

"Oh, in half an hour. I'll set this one right
in the window so it will be ready sooner."

The Dana girls helped to tidy the kitchen.
They had just completed the task when the
front doorbell rang. Jean answered it, and
returned a minute later with a sealed envelope
which she handed to Mrs. Doke.

"I found this on the porch," she said.

"Oh, dear, it's probably another message
from that dreadful man, John Ely!"

Frowning, Mrs. Doke went into the living
room to find her spectacles. She sat down and
carefully read the note before handing it to the
Dana girls.

"Yes, it's just as I thought. Only this time
he is much more threatening."

"How many notes has John Ely sent you?"
Jean questioned curiously.

"Six in all."

"Yet he never comes to see you in person."

"No, that's the queer part of it. I wasn't
too much worried at first, but lately I've begun
to wonder if I've made a grave mistake."

"By giving away the money?" Jean asked.

"Yes. This man Ely threatens to sue me
unless I turn over the contents of the chest to
him within the next twenty-four hours. Of
course, I couldn't do that if I wanted to for

part of the money has already been distributed.''

''You are in an awkward situation,'' Louise agreed.

''I only did what I thought was right—what Mason told me to do. But lately I've been thinking——''

''Yes?'' Jean prompted as the woman hesitated.

''I dislike saying it, but I feel I may speak frankly with you girls. The truth is, I've begun to wonder if Mason didn't lie about that money.''

Jean and Louise did not like to admit that they had been worrying over the same thing. They remained silent.

''If I've given away money belonging to John Ely he can have me sent to prison,'' Mrs. Doke continued nervously. ''I'd be unable to plead innocence for I've received many warnings from him.''

''No one could blame you for refusing to deal with a man whom you have never seen,'' Louise commented. ''I shouldn't worry over this note if I were you, Mrs. Doke. It's probably a bluff like all the others.''

''I sincerely hope so.''

The three discussed the matter for a time; then Jean arose and went to the kitchen to see if the apple pie for Miss McKinley had cooled.

A moment later Louise and Mrs. Doke heard her muttering to herself.

"What's wrong, Sis?" Louise called.

"Just come here and see for yourself!" Jean urged in a baffled tone. "Unless I'm imagining things, the pie is gone!"

CHAPTER XXI

The Treasure Hunt

"If that boy of mine has been around the yard, I think I can explain the mystery of the missing pie," Mrs. Doke remarked, grimly surveying the empty window ledge.

"Joe was batting a tennis ball out by the garage only a few minutes ago," Jean said.

"Then I fear he's the guilty person."

Mrs. Doke sternly called her son into the house. He was so amazed at the accusation that no one could doubt but that he spoke the truth in saying that he had not touched the apple pie.

"Maybe Daisy or Belle ate it up," he suggested.

"I never allow them to eat pie," Mrs. Doke replied. "No, I'd quicker think a tramp took it from the shelf."

In truth, Joe's theory was very nearly correct. Only a few minutes earlier Daisy and Belle had noticed the pastry in the window. They had remembered their mother's admonition not to eat it, but could see no reason why they should not play "market."

Taking the pie from the window, they had placed it in an old basket which they had found in the yard. Then, unobserved, they had wandered off down the street, launched upon their "shopping."

While the group in the house was exclaiming over the missing pie, a car turned into the driveway just at that moment. It came to a standstill in front of the garage.

"Why, it's Aunt Harriet!" Louise cried, running to greet her.

"I thought I might find you girls here at this hour," Miss Dana laughed as she alighted. "I brought you a dressed chicken, Mrs. Doke. I had to have an excuse for calling, you know."

"Indeed, you need none," Mrs. Doke smilingly contradicted. "You are always welcome here. Today we're particularly eager to see you. We need your advice."

"I always enjoy giving that," Miss Dana chuckled.

"I received another message from John Ely today," Mrs. Doke explained. "He gives me just twenty-four hours in which to turn over the money to him."

"May I see the note?"

"Of course. Do come into the house. Louise will get it while I slip this chicken into the ice box. It was very good of you to bring it."

By the time Mrs. Doke emerged from the

kitchen Miss Dana had finished reading the message.

"My advice to you, Mrs. Doke, is to get a lawyer at once," she said.

"But Aunt Harriet," Jean protested, "if the matter is turned over to an attorney the entire story must be revealed."

"Lawyers cost money," Mrs. Doke commented uneasily. "They always seem to involve one in a suit."

"I think Jean and I can solve this mystery if we have a few days more," Louise interposed quickly. "There are many angles to the case. We've just started to work on it."

"For that matter, we've really never made a thorough search of this house to learn if any other boxes are secreted here," Jean added. "It seems to me we should do that some time soon."

"Let's explore now!" Joe proposed enthusiastically. "I know a dandy place to start, too!"

"Where?" Louise inquired, smiling.

"In the cellar. That's where we found the chest of money."

"I doubt if we'll unearth anything more there," Jean said. "I was about to suggest the attic myself."

"That's where I think you should look," Aunt Harriet agreed.

"We might all pitch in and make a complete job of it," Louise laughed. "Joe can dig in the cellar. Jean and I will pry up the boards in the various closets. Aunt Harriet and Mrs. Doke can explore the attic."

"What a wreck the place will be when we finish," Miss Dana commented. "Mrs. Doke may not care to have her house all torn up."

"Oh, I've intended to make a complete search for many days. I'll be grateful if you will help me."

"Here I go to the cellar!" Joe cried in high glee. "I'll be the one to find the money, too! You'll see!"

While Aunt Harriet and Mrs. Doke went to the attic armed with flashlights, broom and dustpan, Louise and Jean began work on the flooring of the closets. After an hour's labor they grew slightly discouraged.

"I'm tired of this," Louise announced. "I think I'll investigate the built-in bookcase just to rest my back."

She crossed over to a huge cabinet which occupied nearly half of one side of the living room. The shelves were crowded with books. Louise removed some of them so that she might run her hand behind the rows. Her exploring fingers touched a folded paper. Quickly she drew it forth.

"Jean, I've found something!" she cried.

"Why, it's nothing but an old insurance policy which ran out years ago!"

"I guess you're right," Louise admitted sheepishly.

She finished searching through the bookcase but discovered nothing of further interest. However, a call from the attic caused the girls to hurry there, hopeful that either Mrs. Doke or Aunt Harriet might have made an important find.

"Just look at this!" Miss Dana proudly held up two China figures which she had salvaged from an old box. "Mrs. Doke has given them to me. Aren't they clever?"

"Aunt Harriet, you're not engaged in an antique hunt!" Jean chided. "We're supposed to be looking for treasure."

"Don't deprive me of my simple pleasures," Miss Dana laughed. "I'm really afraid the attic has no treasure to give up. We've searched it from top to bottom. I've peered into everything except that big cupboard. I'll get the step ladder and go after it now."

Louise and Jean returned to the lower floor to finish their own work. Scarcely had they left the attic than they heard a loud thud, followed by Aunt Harriet's excited scream.

"Now what?" Jean demanded in alarm.

"Maybe she found another China figure."

"And smashed it to bits."

They raced up the stairway two steps at a time. Flinging open the attic door, they beheld their aunt lying in an ungainly heap on the floor, pinned down by the overturned step ladder. She was laughing hilariously, with Mrs. Doke trying to assist her to arise. This was a difficult task, for Miss Dana was clutching a small box tightly in both hands and could not help herself.

"Are you hurt, Aunt Harriet?" Jean cried anxiously.

"Not a bit, or I shouldn't be laughing. I found this box, and in my excitement I fell off the step ladder."

"You should have dropped the box and tried to save yourself, Aunt Harriet," Louise chided. "You might have been seriously injured."

"I didn't have time to think about that," Miss Dana confessed as she struggled to her feet. "Well, since I've caused so much commotion let's see what's inside the box. It's as heavy as lead."

Mrs. Doke and the girls gathered eagerly about her. She fumbled with the catch and finally lifted the lid. Everyone gasped in awe. The box was filled to capacity with gleaming yellow coins.

"Gold!" Mrs. Doke exclaimed.

"There must be at least five hundred dollars," Jean declared.

"Oh, far more than that," Louise corrected. "I'd say nearer a thousand."

Eagerly the group fell to counting the money. Louise had made the better guess. The box contained one thousand and fifty dollars.

"Will John Ely claim this money too, I wonder?" Mrs. Doke questioned, thinking aloud.

"We'll trust he never learns of it," Jean answered. "At least, the box isn't marked with his name."

In all the excitement everyone had forgotten about Joe, who was still digging in the cellar, hopeful of being the one to find the treasure. When Louise was on the point of calling him he came clattering up the stairs. His eyes fairly bulged at sight of the gold, and he asked so many eager questions that no one could answer them all.

"Joe," his mother said suddenly, "where are the children?"

"Why, I don't know," the boy replied in surprise. "I thought they were up here with you."

"No, I haven't seen them since we started this search."

"Very likely they're playing contentedly in the yard," Louise remarked as she saw that Mrs. Doke was getting worried.

"I saw no one when I drove up in the car," Aunt Harriet contributed.

Mrs. Doke ran to the attic window and called loudly. The yard was deserted and there was no answer.

"The children are gone!" cried their mother. "Oh, I've been so careless not to have watched them closer. I don't know whatever possessed me—I was thinking about the treasure, I guess."

"Try to keep calm, Mrs. Doke," Aunt Harriet said kindly. "Daisy and Belle can't have strayed far. We'll find them in a few minutes."

They hastened to the street, the Dana girls trying to bolster up Mrs. Doke's courage by assuming their aunt's optimism; yet they were dismayed to notice how low the sun had sunk toward the western horizon.

"It will soon be dark," Jean whispered to her sister. "If we don't find them before night——"

"Oh, we will," Louise returned. "Don't look so alarmed, Jean."

"But I'm afraid——"

"Afraid! Of what?"

Jean darted a glance at Mrs. Doke to make certain that the woman was not within hearing distance. Then she answered, very low:

"Kidnapers!"

CHAPTER XXII

A Question of Ransom

WITHIN three quarters of an hour the streets were shrouded in shadows. Still Daisy and Belle had not been found.

Mrs. Doke went from house to house inquiring if anyone had seen the children. Finally she collapsed from worry. Aunt Harriet ministered to the distraught woman, while Louise and Jean, assisted by kindly neighbors, continued the search.

By this time everyone had begun to fear that the little girls had been kidnaped. Accordingly there was great rejoicing when Louise and Jean obtained their first useful clue. A woman several blocks away from the Doke home reported that she had seen the children pass her house nearly two hours before, carrying a market basket.

The Dana girls canvassed other persons in the district, gleaning scattered bits of information. They were able to trail the children toward the edge of town.

From a watchman at a railroad crossing they received their most useful, yet most disturbing, tip. He recalled that two little girls, answering the description of Daisy and Belle, had passed the crossing just at sundown, accompanied by a man.

"How was he dressed?" Louise inquired.

"He wore a dark suit. A felt hat was pulled low over his eyes, so I could catch only a glimpse of his face."

"Which way did he take the children?" Jean questioned.

"I noticed that they walked down the track for a short distance, then cut across into the woods. The man seemed to be half dazed, for after he left the railroad right of way he staggered about and didn't seem to know where he wanted to go."

Jean and Louise exchanged brief glances. It occurred to them both that the man they were trailing might be the masked stranger who had displayed the strange characteristic of moving in circles.

Thanking the watchman for the information, the girls hastened along the tracks toward the woods. They found the place where the children and their mysterious companion had left the right of way, for little Daisy had dropped her handkerchief in the weeds.

"And here are footprints!" Louise exclaimed. "They make a wide circle and then lead toward the woods!"

There was no need to measure the prints, for the Danas saw at a glance that they belonged to the mysterious stranger. The girls were more fearful than ever now that the man had kidnaped Daisy and Belle.

Louise and Jean followed the trail into the woods, but it was impossible for them to keep to it in the gathering darkness. At length, convinced that they were just wasting precious time, the girls hastened back to the Doke cottage to report their findings.

During their absence Aunt Harriet had put Mrs. Doke to bed. The woman became hysterical when she learned that the Dana girls had uncovered evidence of kidnaping, and could not be calmed until a physician administered a sedative, which put her to sleep.

During the night sympathetic neighbors, directed by the Dana girls, searched the woods by the light of lanterns and torches. No trace of the children could be found; only another baffling circle of footprints near the river's edge.

"It looks like a case of kidnaping," Louise acknowledged wearily the next morning. She was seated with her sister at the Doke breakfast table, drinking coffee which Aunt Harriet had prepared for all the weary searchers. "By this time that man has gone into hiding."

Jean nodded gloomily. "Will there be a demand for ransom, I wonder?" she mused.

"Probably for the entire amount Mrs. Doke has in her possession!"

"Oh, Mrs. Doke requested me to speak to you about that," Aunt Harriet said quickly. "She wants you girls to go to the bank as soon as it opens this morning and bring back all the rest of her money."

"But would that be wise?" Jean questioned doubtfully.

"Mrs. Doke wishes to have the funds on hand in case the demand for ransom is received to-day."

"Then she intends to pay it without question or delay?" Louise asked.

"Oh, yes, the poor woman is half out of her mind with worry. She will turn over every penny in her possession to secure the safe return of her children."

"One can't blame her for that," Louise responded, "but I feel we're dealing with a wily criminal just now. We can't move too carefully."

"It will only upset Mrs. Doke if you refuse to do her errand. I myself feel that it would be wise to leave it in the bank until the ransom demand is received, but after all, the funds do belong to Mrs. Doke. She has a right to make her own decisions about them."

At nine o'clock Louise and Jean presented themselves at the bank, and under escort carried the money to Mrs. Doke. The latter was confident that a demand for ransom would be received that day but the hours dragged on and no word came. Aunt Harriet and the girls had suggested that the police be called in to aid in the search for Daisy and Belle. Despite her great anxiety, Mrs. Doke would not agree.

"If we bring the police into the affair the kidnaper may never communicate with us," she insisted.

Jean and Louise were unwilling to sit idle. They combed the woods and even searched the cave where the treasure originally had been hidden. Chancing to encounter Herman Waite they enlisted his aid, but he had no success whatever in picking up the trail of the kidnaper.

"I'm dreadfully afraid the children were stolen in revenge by that masked robber," Jean commented unhappily, as she and her sister trudged wearily back to the Doke cottage at the end of the day.

"Perhaps a message has been received from him during our absence," Louise expressed hopefully. "Here comes Joe to meet us now, and he seems excited."

The boy ran toward the girls, waving a piece of white paper in his hand.

"Is it from the kidnaper?" Jean demanded eagerly.

Joe shook his head. "No, from your uncle—Captain Dana. He's coming here today."

"Why, I had no idea Uncle Ned's ship was in port!" Louise exclaimed.

"He's coming with a couple of visitors—

"Julia Bellington!" Jean cried in elation. "Mr. Riley finally located her!"

Then the light faded from her face. It occurred to her that the woman was making the trip to the Doke cottage expecting to receive the four thousand dollars due her. In the present emergency she wondered if Mrs. Doke would be willing to give up the funds which might be required to secure the release of Daisy and Belle. Certainly Miss Bellington had been located at an awkward time.

After reading the brief note from their uncle, the girls entered the house. Mrs. Doke, pale and haggard, sat by the window, awaiting their arrival.

"No news of my babies?" she asked in a strained voice.

Louise was compelled to reply that they had none. While the girls were endeavoring to cheer Mrs. Doke, a taxi drew up in front of the house. From the kitchen Aunt Harriet called out that her brother had arrived with the expected guests.

The Dana girls rushed out to greet the newcomers. They paused in delighted amazement as they saw Mr. Riley slowly alight from the cab.

"Behold!" he called gaily, "the old invalid has thrown away his hated wheel chair and crutches!"

"Oh, it's wonderful!" Jean cried. "And you look years younger, Mr. Riley! A sea voyage was just the thing you needed."

An attractive woman with golden hair and pleasant blue eyes had stepped from the taxi to stand quietly by Mr. Riley's side. The latter proudly introduced the girls to Julia Bellington, adding that she had consented to marry him within a few weeks.

"I've never been so happy in all my life," he confessed. "My good fortune began the day you two girls called at my home. Now that I have found Julia, my life can never be empty or dreary again."

"We owe so much to you," Miss Bellington added, her face radiant. "I can't tell you how grateful I am—for everything. I assure you I was dazed when I learned that I was to receive four thousand dollars. I've decided to use part of it to buy a trousseau."

Louise and Jean lowered their eyes and could find nothing to say. Captain Dana, who had been a silent spectator to the little drama, divined instantly that something was amiss, but Miss Bellington chatted gaily on.

"I don't wish to seem grasping," she laughed, "but I do hope Mrs. Doke has my check ready for me. I've waited so many years for that money!"

CHAPTER XXIII

A Vague Clue

As Mr. Riley and Miss Bellington walked slowly toward the house, Captain Dana dropped back a pace to speak quietly with his nieces.

"Anything wrong?" he inquired.

"Just about everything," Jean replied soberly. "Mrs. Doke's children have been kidnaped."

"Things are in a hopeless muddle," Louise added. "Mrs. Doke won't notify the police, and now Miss Bellington's arrival complicates the money situation."

"Not that it wasn't complicated before," Jean interposed grimly. "John Ely has entered the picture, too. He claims the funds which were found in the chest."

Captain Dana whistled softly, his shaggy brows puckering into a troubled frown.

"I guess it's a good thing I came home," he commented. "This affair seems to call for drastic action."

The Dana girls were not mistaken in assuming that Mrs. Doke would be reluctant to

198

give away the money which had been turned over to her by her husband. Although the woman was happy that Miss Bellington had been located, she was afraid to part with the four thousand dollars lest the sum be required to help meet a ransom demand.

Miss Bellington, though visibly disappointed, accepted the decision with excellent grace. "Of course I don't blame you, Mrs. Doke," she said. "Your children must come first. If there is anything Mr. Riley and I can do to help you, don't hesitate to call upon us."

"I fear there is nothing anyone can do until we hear from the kidnapers," Mrs. Doke answered dispiritedly.

This was Captain Dana's opportunity to speak his mind.

"It seems to me, Mrs. Doke," he said, "that there is a great deal to be done. In my opinion, you are making a grave mistake by withholding the information of the kidnaping from the police."

So strongly did he urge the matter, that after the others had echoed the advice Mrs. Doke reluctantly agreed that the police might be notified. Captain Dana and his nieces went immediately to the Penfield station where all clues in the case were turned over to the authorities.

In returning to the Doke cottage, the three

drove along a busy street. Suddenly Louise gripped her uncle's arm and pointed out to him a bent old woman in a faded blue bonnet. She was buying vegetables at a vendor's stall.

"There she is now, Uncle Ned! Miss Mc-Kinley—we were telling you about her, you know."

They halted the car at the curbing to watch the woman's movements. Captain Dana suggested that he alight and speak with her for a moment, but Jean and Louise dissuaded him.

"It would only create a scene," the latter insisted. "She really isn't responsible for what she does or says."

Miss McKinley finished her marketing and continued down the street with the heavily laden basket on her arm.

"She seems to be buying considerable produce," Louise remarked as they drove on again toward the Doke cottage. "I wonder how she uses up so much, living by herself?"

"The cupboard was bare enough when we were at her house," Jean recalled.

"Yes, it was. That's why it seems strange that she should go on this sudden orgy of spending."

Although the Dana girls felt relieved that the police had taken up the search for little Daisy and Belle, they had no intention of lessening their own efforts. Aided by Uncle

Ned, Mr. Riley and Miss Bellington, they searched the countryside, visited abandoned houses, and interviewed hundreds of persons.

Professor and Mrs. Crandall, chagrined because their nephew had been involved in dishonest dealings, were more than eager to assist Mrs. Doke. They organized the girls from the Starhurst School into squads, sending them out to search the woods in systematic fashion. No trace of the missing children was found, however.

"There's one clue we may have overlooked," Louise said thoughtfully to her sister after another twenty-four hours had elapsed. "It's just possible Algernon Prentice may know something about this kidnaping."

"You think he would steal the children?"

"No, but he may be able to provide us with a clue. It will do no harm to ask him about it."

That afternoon the girls drove to the colored man's cabin. He was not at home, but after considerable trouble they located him working at a nearby farm. Algernon Prentice did not look any too pleased to see the girls, doubtless fearing that they had come to annoy him again about the stolen perfume.

Jean did not know what angle of questioning her sister intended to pursue. She was a little surprised when Louise asked Algernon if he had ever met a colored man by the name of

John Ely. Algernon scratched his tousled head thoughtfully, then gave a negative answer.

"Have you ever heard of anyone by that name?" Louise persisted. "Think hard, Algernon."

" 'Deed now, seems to me I did hear ole Missy McKinley say somethin' 'bout a white man named Ely. Or maybe it was Doke. I can't just recollect."

"Doke?" Louise demanded eagerly. "Oh, Algernon, try to recall what Miss McKinley said about them."

"I neveh paid much 'tention to what she did say. Ole Missy was always ramblin' on 'bout havin' dark secrets. Seems like she had one with this Ely—'bout money. Mis' McKinley was funny 'bout money, yas'm. I won't w'uk foh her nò mo' since she quit payin' me."

In vain the girls tried to glean additional information. Algernon had told them all he knew and Jean was inclined to believe that possibly he had made up some of it, just to be done with the questioning.

"We can't afford to overlook any clue," Louise commented after the girls had left the farm. "I propose that we visit Miss McKinley again and probe deeper into any connection of hers with John Ely."

"I'm willing for you to do the probing, Louise!"

"I don't relish another interview myself, but if we learn she has valuable information we can turn the woman over to the police. They'll be able to deal with her."

The girls went directly to Miss McKinley's home. There was no sign of movement about the place. All the doors were closed and nearly all the shades were pulled down.

"Shall we knock?" Jean questioned.

"Not just yet. It will only excite Miss McKinley. I want to look inside first. Here's one shade she forgot to pull down."

Louise indicated a window at the rear of the house. It was far above the level of their heads, but Jean found an old box upon which they could stand. Louise cautiously peered through the glass.

Jean, who was offering her sister support by holding her hand, felt the girl's muscles grow taut. Louise stood as one turned to stone, staring blankly into the dim interior of the old house.

"What do you see?" Jean whispered impatiently. "Tell me!"

CHAPTER XXIV

The Eccentric Housekeeper

"Daisy and Belle!" Louise exclaimed in a voice so low that it was almost inaudible. "They're playing in Miss McKinley's sitting room!"

She quickly stepped down from the box so that her sister might take her place. Jean peered eagerly through the window and saw for herself that the children appeared unharmed. They were contentedly munching cookies and cake.

Before either of the girls could comment upon their discovery, an upstairs window flew open and Miss McKinley wrathfully gazed down upon them.

"Snoopers!" she screamed. "Go away, or else come to the front door and knock! I won't have you peering into my windows!"

"We're sorry," Louise apologized instantly. "Of course we'll come to the door as you request."

Feeling rather elated that an entry was to be accomplished so easily, the Dana girls hastened to the front of the house. As they

stood waiting to be admitted, they had no suspicion that Miss McKinley had gone directly to
the kitchen, there to "doctor" a plate of cake
with a small portion of the rat poison which
she had purchased some days before.

To Daisy and Belle the demented woman
said hastily, "We are about to have visitors.
When they come you must be polite and offer
them some of your chocolate cake. The cake on
this blue plate. Not the other."

Unaware of the plot, Jean and Louise diffi-
dently entered the house.

"I suppose you came here to rob and steal?"
Miss McKinley said in a shrill tone.

"Indeed, we didn't," Jean answered soothingly. "We came on two important missions.
First, to inquire why you are keeping these
two little girls in your house——"

"I'm not keeping them," Miss McKinley interrupted. "They came to my door hungry and
tired. I gave them cake and——"

"A man sent us here," Belle chimed in.
"He said this was the house where we were to
come."

"Keep still, will you?" irate Miss McKinley
snapped.

Frightened by her tone, Daisy and Belle ran
to the Dana girls, clinging tightly to them.

"Was it a nice man who sent you here,
darling?" Jean gently questioned little Belle.

The child merely stared, unable to reply. Daisy, forgetting her fear, shyly picked up the blue plate filled with chocolate cake and offered it to Louise.

"No, honey, not now," Louise declined absently. "You eat it."

A look of disappointment came over Miss McKinley's face as the child returned the plate to the table. Louise and Jean noticed the expression but could not interpret its significance.

They were eager to leave the house as quickly as possible with Daisy and Belle, yet they feared that Miss McKinley would create a scene unless they handled her most diplomatically. Cautiously Louise began to question the woman concerning John Ely.

"You want to know entirely too much!" Miss McKinley flared suddenly.

"I'll give you four thousand dollars if you'll answer my questions," Louise proposed, inspired by a spur-of-the-moment plan. Four thousand was exactly the sum due Miss McKinley from Mrs. Doke.

A crafty light came into the demented woman's smoldering eyes.

"Show me the money and maybe I'll tell you what you want to know."

"We haven't it with us," Louise was forced to reply. "We can bring it when we come again."

"Then I'll answer your questions the next time, too."

"If we are to give you the money, you must tell us about John Ely now," Jean urged.

Miss McKinley hesitated, seemingly tempted to make an important revelation. At that moment a black crow fluttered against the window pane. Then it flew into the room.

"An evil omen!" the demented woman shrieked. "It is a sign that I must reveal nothing. Not a word will I tell you of John Ely or how he died! You shall never hear about the insurance money, either! Oh! Oh! Get that wicked bird out of here!"

Jean and Louise made an attempt to corner the crow but it fluttered wildly about the room. Finally it perched itself on a desk, picking up an old letter in its beak.

Jean crept softly toward the bird. She reached out to snatch it from its perch, but the crow flew away again. However, in its fright it dropped the piece of paper. Jean reached down and picked it up.

"It's mine!" Miss McKinley proclaimed shrilly. "I've written everything out about John Ely. You're not to read it!"

Jean looked questioningly at her sister.

"It's our only chance of learning the truth," Louise said in an undertone. "Read it while I watch Miss McKinley."

Jean pretended to put down the sheet, but while Louise drew the woman's attention toward the children, she scanned the cramped writing, her face mirroring varied emotions. In a rational moment Miss McKinley had revealed on the paper the strange details of her life as housekeeper for John Ely. For ten years she had served him despite her knowledge that the man was a crook. She had remained in his service because of the high wages paid her, but in time he had grown to begrudge her the sum. When he had ceased to remunerate her at all, Miss McKinley had stayed on, having no other place to go.

The housekeeper had deeply resented her employer's attitude, particularly since she had surmised that with the aid of Peter Short and Mason Doke, who served as tools, he had stolen what amounted to a fortune from various victims. By threats she had induced Ely to sign an insurance policy over to her in lieu of wages. One day her employer accidentally took poison which Miss McKinley had kept for household purposes in an old salt shaker. Although no one blamed the housekeeper for Ely's death, his demise had preyed upon her mind, and she had lived in constant fear that she would be accused of having poisoned him to gain his insurance.

"Read the rest later!" Louise warned her

sister. "A man is coming up the path to the house."

Jean hastily secreted the paper in her pocket. By this time the visitor had emerged from among the pine trees. He walked with unsteady gait and slowly made a wide circle be-, fore approaching the front door.

"It's the mysterious stranger!" Jean whispered in awe. "Only now he isn't wearing his mask."

"Peter Short!" exclaimed Miss McKinley. "What's he want now?"

"Of course he's the one who has pretended to Mrs. Doke that he was John Ely," Jean guessed shrewdly. "That day we saw him in the woods he had blackened his face."

The girls knew that they would have to act quickly if they were to trap the man. They would never have another opportunity. Miss McKinley presented a grave problem, but she seemed quiet enough. At least she made no outcry as Louise snatched up a long scarf from the table.

The girls huddled by the door. When the man rapped sharply Louise opened it, keeping out of sight. Then Peter Short stepped into the room.

Louise and Jean sprang from their hiding place, and before the man was aware of their presence, they had pinned his arms behind him.

Then they securely tied him with the scarf.

Peter Short struggled furiously, but the girls succeeded in drawing the knots tighter and tighter. However, before they had completely subdued him Miss McKinley began to weep hysterically.

"Try to quiet her," Louise directed Jean.

"I won't be quiet! I won't!" Miss McKinley screamed. "Only if you eat the chocolate cake."

"What has that to do with it?" Jean asked blankly.

"Oh, do anything to humor her. We must stop this racket."

Jean reached for a piece of the cake, nibbling at it.

"Both of you must eat it!" Miss McKinley chortled. "Both of you!"

"Oh, all right." Impatiently Louise crossed the room and selected a slice. She took several bites.

"Girls like chocolate cake," Miss McKinley chuckled gloatingly. "That's what the bakery woman said!"

The cake slipped from Jean's fingers, crumbling upon the floor. Her face had grown pasty in color.

"Louise, does that cake—taste funny to you?"

Miss McKinley rocked back and forth in her chair, laughing hysterically.

Jean reached out to grip the table for support. She felt wretchedly ill. Louise could not go to her, for she, too, had been stricken.

"We've been poisoned," she whispered hoarsely. "Miss McKinley tricked us."

CHAPTER XXV

A Final Settlement

Too ill to think of anything save their own intense suffering, Louise and Jean staggered from the house, followed by the terrified Doke children.

"Go—for—help," Jean gasped, sinking to the ground.

Belle and Daisy raced off through the pine grove with no clear idea of what was wrong. Happily for the Dana girls, Joe Doke had been searching for his sisters in that very vicinity and was walking slowly along the road. He joyfully rushed to his sisters, and they tearfully told him of the strange way Louise and Jean had acted after eating Miss McKinley's cake.

Joe was starting at a run for the insane woman's house when Herman Waite chanced to pass in his new automobile. The boy hailed him, tersely explaining that the Dana girls were in trouble.

"Jump in," Mr. Waite ordered.

The car rattled up the winding lane, jerking to a halt near the house. Joe and Mr. Waite found the two victims lying on the lawn, moaning.

"Water!" Louise pleaded.

Joe ran into the house to get it. The place was deserted, for Miss McKinley, horrified by her own sinister deed, had fled to the woods. Peter Short too had managed to free himself and escape.

Joe raced back with water and the girls were given all they could drink. Mr. Waite and he then lifted them into the automobile, driving with all speed to the nearest hospital, where Louise and Jean were given emergency treatment. By the time Aunt Harriet and Uncle Ned, summoned by Joe, arrived upon the scene, the girls were slowly recovering from the attack.

"Fortunately they did not take a great deal of the poison into their systems," the doctor explained to Miss Dana. "But even so, they owe their lives to the fact that they were rushed directly to the hospital."

That evening there was great rejoicing in the Doke cottage. Mrs. Doke was fairly beside herself with joy at the return of Daisy and Belle, yet she could not help but feel apprehensive because Peter Short remained at large.

Louise and Jean, released from the hospital, wasted no time in placing their evidence in the hands of police. Officers went immediately to the old house in the pine grove only to find that Peter Short and the housekeeper had fled. They were unable to pick up Short's trail. Later that evening, however, Miss McKinley was discovered wandering aimlessly about in the woods.

Questioned by skilled psychiatrists, she readily admitted the poison plot against the Dana girls, and gave an account of her life with John Ely, which was incoherent, but had items similar to the written account which Jean had taken and handed over to the police. This left no doubt as to the manner in which the man had gained the fortune found in the Doke home.

Several days elapsed before police were able to trace Peter Short. They received their first clue when a masked man robbed a filling station located on the edge of the city. A circle of footprints threw suspicion upon Short. A police net was spread in the vicinity, and within twenty-four hours the fellow was apprehended. He pleaded guilty to the various charges against him, and received a long prison sentence.

Mrs. Doke could not praise the Dana girls enough for the aid they had given her in settling her husband's tangled affairs. With all the old debts repaid, including the sum due Miss Bellington, a fairly large amount of money remained undistributed.

When a court officially awarded the funds to Mrs. Doke to be used by her in rearing her little family, the grateful woman wanted to reward Louise and Jean in a material way. They firmly refused to accept a penny, however, declaring that they had been fully compensated by bringing happiness to so many deserving persons.

If the Dana girls thought they were to escape without any tangible expression of gratitude from their many new friends, they were greatly mistaken. It fell to the lot of Casey Riley to think of a way to pay them homage.

Louise and Jean were asked to a dinner served at his mansion in their honor. When they arrived at the Riley home with Aunt Harriet and Uncle Ned, the girls were delighted to greet not only their kind host and his fiancee, Julia Bellington, but a group of other persons connected with the Doke case. Herman Waite, Mr. and Mrs. Judson, Samuel Slayback, Mrs. Tito and her talented daughter, and Mrs. Doke with Joe, completed the list of guests.

After dinner had been served everyone gathered in the music room, where Miss Tito and Joe Doke entertained with piano and flute selections. Later, when they were all in the drawing room, the Dana girls were obliged to answer many questions about the strange case which had brought restitution to so many of

the guests.   Their interrogators were especially interested in the apprehension of Peter
Short and the sinister part he had played in
attempting to impersonate the deceased John
Ely. It was brought out that the man had once
been a sailor and walked with a rolling gait.
In times of stress he had an eccentric habit of
going in circles until he made up his mind what
to do. These two facts accounted for the circles
or part circles of footprints which he left.

"To my knowledge, there's one mystery connected with this affair which remains unex-
plained," Captain Dana remarked lightly.
"How did you girls manage to keep from failing
in your classes?"

"I think Professor and Mrs. Crandall favored
us a bit," Jean laughed. "But from now on
we'll devote all our time to studies."

"Until the next adventure knocks at your
dormitory door," the man chuckled.

How true his prophecy was would be shown
when the sisters were to be invited on a camp-
ing trip and solve "The Mystery of the Locked
Room."

"Knowing you both so well," Uncle Ned went
on, "I'm afraid you wouldn't be entirely happy
unless you were unraveling the threads of some
mystery."

"And we're afraid you're right," laughed his
nieces gaily.

THE END